Surreal Eternity

A Novel by

Gary Stewart Branfman

Dear Ms. Yates –

Enjoy!

TurnKey press

Surreal Eternity

"Surreal Eternity" cover painting. Oil on masonite,
by Sarah Yuster
www.zographia.com

ISBN: 0-9740030-3-4

2525 W Anderson Lane, Suite 540
Austin, Texas 78757

Tel: 512.407.8876
Fax: 512.478.2117

E-mail: info@turnkeypress.com
Web: www.turnkeypress.com

To my three graces, Sarah, Shaina, and Hannah,
and to Susan: my wife, my friend and my muse.

In memory of my mother.

"A baby is God's opinion
that the world should go on."

-Carl Sandburg

Prologue

As Muhammed awakened he glanced over at Carole. Still stunning past forty, his bride of one year was a woman he loved with his heart, mind, and soul. Four years her junior, Muhammed Hassan viewed her stunning profile and thick, flowing hair.

As she stretched and she yawned, the sun's brilliant rays gazed. The dawn and Muhammed gave thanks to Allah for her breathtaking features and radiant glow. She needed neither make-up nor trips to salons. Her inherent beauty and natural charm surpassed that of her peers all made up, in fine gowns.

Opening her eyes, she sighed, "What time is it, hon?" Carole squinted and smiled, and then closed her eyes.

At that moment, a voice on her clock radio said, "And a beautiful morning it is here in New York City at seven thirty-five a.m."

Wedged between Carole and her husband was their dazzling six-year old, Aneesa. Hugging their daughter with paramount affection, they painted unparalleled smiles of bliss on a canvas of Neil Diamond's "September Morn'."

To the casual observer, this tall, bearded Arab and his beautiful Jewish wife might have seemed poles apart. The casual observer would have been dead wrong. The innate understanding and passion they shared was a gift only God could have conceived.

Before their paths had crossed, they had each chose another to love and to cherish until death due them part. They never anticipated how soon death would intervene. On one heart-wrenching day six years before, their fates and their faiths would collide.

1

Seagulls in the Mist

Beneath bald cypress trees and overcast skies, the cemetery over flowed with rivers of tears. Etched granite stones on dormant grass and icy concrete walking paths led mourners to the gravesite.

A row of wooden folding chairs sat upon a frozen rug, sheltered from the chilling drizzle by a canvas awning overhead.

A wife, two sons, and four grandparents took their seats like granite blocks. The casket sunk beneath the hard cold ground to sounds of Hebrew prayers.

Like a stone tossed on a silent pond, wave upon wave of family and peers rippled across the crowded lawn as Dr. Meyer was laid to rest after an all too short 41 years.

Dr. Meyer had been jogging along the beachfront drive, just like a thousand times before. While breathing the brisk salty ocean air, the winter's sun glared through dense fog, highlighting his hair and obscuring his view. In a runner's trance, he did not notice the approaching instrument of his death.

His mind's final image was a swerving red car. The screeching crescendo of racing car brakes was in sync with screaming seagulls in the mist. His death was immediate and painless.

His widowed wife Carole glared down at the coffin in catatonic disbelief. She was oblivious to the Rabbi's last prayers as voices echoed in her mind.

"Would his eyelids now forever hide his tantalizing deep blue eyes?"

Had Salvador Dali imprisoned her in a static surreal eternity?

Mrs. Meyer spoke, though her lips barely moved. "But he just went out for a jog. Just to relax. Just to stay fit. It was just a short jog."

When the service ended, a black limousine shuttled the family down a wide tree-lined street. They arrived at the Meyer's Long Island estate and were greeted by heads bowing down, bathed in tears. Carole, her sons, and her parents stepped down from the car. Soggy leaves softened the ground for their feet and the fresh scent of firewood welcomed them home. Mrs. Meyer, David and Andrew approached the entrance ahead of the rest.

Picasso would have savored the abstract reflection of their blue twisted faces on century-old glass as they opened the ornate hand-carved double doors.

Mahogany walls flanked cathedral ceilings and a long winding staircase reached up toward the sky. High overhead was a massive glass dome, dividing the earth from the heavens above.

Déjà vu seized Carole and sucked her into the room. Three decades before, she had slid down the banister. Both she and her father had been raised in this home that her grandfather built before cars and paved roads.

In a daze now, she was in another time. A happier time.

Carole's grandfather, Dr. Charles W. Cohen, was a dinosaur from a dying breed of physicians. On the verge of extinction, he had mastered his craft back in "the good old days" of medicine. Aside from his practice, he also contracted with drug research labs helping secure pharmaceutical patents.

For pennies a share he'd purchased their stocks. The wealth he had amassed for his brains and his insight was respected, not envied by patients and peers.

A time long ago, Carole's grandfather had shared with her his secret of life. On her tiptoes she had opened the door to his study, sneaked down the stairs and hid behind a couch.

Grandpa Charlie sat at his big wooden desk and swiveled around like a child at play. His thick gray head of hair always sported a skullcap, on top of which a derby proudly sat. Round glasses sat on the end of his bulbous-tipped nose.

"Why are we here, Carole?"

She crawled out of hiding, jumped up on his desk and said: "What do you mean, Grandpa?"

"Why do you think God put us here?"

She leaped from the desk, put her hands behind her back and with a puzzled expression, looked up into his eyes. "Why? Why?"

He cupped his hands around her ear and whispered, "We are here for two reasons. Contribute something good to the world, and at the same time try to have some fun."

She always remembered these few simple words that were whispered to her such a long time ago.

Carole sat motionless by the warmth of the fire and watched the contortions of hypnotic flames. Alone in a vacuum immersed in a crowd, a smile emerged from her grief-ridden face.

She drifted away to an orchestra box at a symphony fund-raiser. Her gown had no back and its silk skimmed her breasts.

Dr. Meyer's moist lips caressed her warm neck as they worked their way up to her ear.

"Your gown is so tempting. Wait until the lights go down, my darling. You're in for a treat."

Although she knew he was teasing, her nipples rose to attention whenever he whispered such words. With magnificence rivaling Grace Kelly's, her casual elegance glowed in the dark. She was as nimble and lean as girls half her age. Her yoga skills thrilled those who saw her contort. Three mornings a week she went to the gym; she could wear out a treadmill while reading a book.

Her eyes filled with tears as a crackling log interrupted her daydream, and halted her joy. Fond memories faded; bright colors turned gray.

She found herself trapped in her large crowded home with muffled sounds slowly becoming distinct: the clicking of glasses, the creaking of doors, a telephone ringing, footsteps strolling by, contrived conversations of whispering mourners, the unyielding wailing of elderly folks.

These piercing sounds swelled to a blaring crescendo. Then silence drowned out the deafening noise. Night fell upon her.

2

Aneesa

On the other side of town stood the Charles Cohen Community Clinic, providing fine healthcare for both rich and poor. This once-prestigious, now-struggling clinic had been hit by the managed care torrential storm.

In medicine's heyday, it had glistened and sang. The wealthy had paid their bills. The less fortunate had paid what they could.

Back in those days, everyone insisted on paying something; it was simply a matter of pride.

When Betty's sore throat felt better, she baby-sat up on the nursery floor. When Mr. Smith's wound was healed, he whitewashed the old clinic fence. Mrs. Johnson's rheumatism didn't stop her from baking great apple pies for the doctors. The system worked. Everyone was cared for. Everyone was happy.

Then breakthroughs in healthcare became daily events, and cure rates for illnesses started to climb. The elderly grew older than ever before and politicians welcomed these wealthy old voters.

"Put Millionaires on Medicare" attracted their votes. When the Medicare System ran out of steam they punished good doctors to take up the slack.

Gang-member dads and their kid's unwed mothers climbed right on board and hitched a free ride. Obstetrics wards gave birth to frivolous lawsuits driving up costs and closing their doors.

Today, the worn-out Community Clinic survives on merciful donations and young doctor's sweat. In spite of its run-down and aging appearance the students who train there are some of the finest.

The doctors who train them are simply "the best."

When an emergency calls, she lifts her head high and stands at attention. There is no trauma for which she is not prepared and no patient to which she would not provide care.

On an icy, rainy winter morning an ambulance pulled up to the emergency-room door. Sirens blasted and red lights flashed.

A woman in labor was rushed to a room as her husband held onto her cold fragile hands. She left a trail of bright red blood in the murky gray slush.

After she whispered some words to her husband, they asked Mr. Hassan to please wait outside. He paced between massive cracking concrete columns where the stench of disease mixed in with the sleet. Graffiti adorned the cold solid wall that he leaned up against with his head in his hands.

Twenty minutes crept by. Then a voice startled him. A woman in scrubs and a bloodstained white lab coat struggled to politely get his attention. He stood in a daze.

"Mr. Muhammed Hassan?"

"Yes. How is she?" he said as a shiver passed through his tall frame.

"Your beautiful seven-pound, five-ounce daughter is waiting to meet her father."

"How is Sabira, my wife?"

When she gave him no answer, he asked to speak with the doctor.

She reached up, placed a delicate hand on his towering shoulder and in a slow soothing voice continued, "Your wife lost too much blood. We did all that we could do. Sabira died a few moments ago. I am so sorry."

His eyes opened wide as he trembled, then froze. Had he been imprisoned in a Dali-esque motionless surreal eternity?

Dr. Marjorie Brennen was a superb physician. Her unequaled toughness could fight off a tiger; her soft inner soul could caress the same beast.

This five-foot-three-inch brunette was intimidating to many but respected by all. In 1965 she'd been born at the clinic and raised in a neighborhood five miles away. High school valedictorian, softball trophy winner, a gifted cellist, and an Ivy League grad.

She was narcissistic, yet good-natured. Her ego always helped her succeed.

She placed a hand on Muhammed's arm and looked into his vacant eyes.

"May I take you to see your Sabira?"

He nodded. Inside, the room was prepared for a family visit. The I.V. had been removed.

Sabira wore a clean sheet and the floor had been mopped, but the bloodstains remained. Dr. Brennen escorted him into the room.

Wordlessly, she asked if he was ready; silently he indicated he was. The doctor stood at his side and pulled the sheet away from the calm lifeless face.

"Take your time Mr. Hassan, I'll wait right outside."

He stared at Sabira's tranquil, closed eyes, lifted her hand for one final touch then kissed her cold forehead, covered her face and walked out. He bowed his head as he spoke to the doctor.

"Would you please take me to see my daughter?"

An awkward stillness accompanied them on the elevator ride to the nursery floor. A bright hallway led them to a colorful room where a dozen new babies checked in for the day.

Dr. Brennen handed Mr. Hassan her card as she said, "My sincere condolences. If there is anything else I can do, please do not hesitate to call me."

Muhammed walked up to the crib, looked at his daughter and burst into tears. She had a full head of black hair and dark, almond-shaped eyes.

He lifted her up, and leaned toward her. As is the custom, Muhammed whispered the call to prayer, *the Adhan*, into Aneesa's right ear, followed by *the Iqamat* into her left. These prayers offer protection and introduce the child to Islam.

He held her tiny body against his muscular chest. He felt her warm heartbeat and she could feel his.

His emotions bounced back and forth between sorrow and joy. His breathing became labored, his pulse raced away and a sudden awareness of gravity frightened him. Her name was Aneesa, the name of his sister who'd died as a child. He placed his newborn back in the crib, stared a while, kissed her, and walked away.

He could not comprehend Allah's unexplained wrath. He was frightened, angered, saddened, numb. He paced with conviction but no destination. Caught in the maze of an Escher illusion without beginning or end.

Outside the cold building, an exhilarating snow flurry greeted him. He wandered upon a small, enclosed garden, which despite the chill oozed a warm Zen-like calm.

Small fragrant bushes and plants with white flowers surrounded a fountain, a sculpture, and smooth concrete benches. Inlaid at their bases in rough textured concrete were several engraved dedicational bricks. He sat on a bench and looked down at a brick. With a blood-stained shoe, he cleared a thin layer of virgin, white snow off a brick, revealing these words:

"A Baby is God's Opinion that the World Should Go On."

Beneath this inscription it said in fine print, "Donated by the Cohen Family for Carole, our new granddaughter."

He sat with his head in his hands as the ravine in his stomach widened. With heartbreaking agony he stood up, took a deep breath, walked into the lobby, reached for the phone and entered the number to Sabira's parents' restaurant.

"It's a good afternoon at Mahshi's," answered his mother-in-law in her thick, joyous, mid-eastern accent. "And how may we be of service today?"

"*Assalaam alaikum*," said Ha-med.

Mrs. Ibrahim detected a sense of distress in his voice. "*Waalaikum Assalaam.* Is everything alright?" she said.

"Congratulations. You have a perfectly flawless seven-and-a-half-pound granddaughter. Aneesa and I will be waiting on the couch in the nursery lounge on the second floor."

The front door sign at Mahshi's was flipped from "open" to "closed." Mr. and Mrs. Ibrahim flew out the door and leapt into their car.

They pulled up to the hospital draped in dirty white aprons. Smiling at each other, they tossed their aprons into the car, joined hands and dashed inside.

The new grandparents ran through the lobby to the elevator. When it opened on the nursery level, they had a clear view of a clearly fatigued Muhammed and Aneesa on the couch.

Scanning for Sabira, they noted her absence and assumed she was resting.

With Aneesa squirming on her father's bare chest, they looked in amazement at God's little gift. They sat down and began a good-natured battle over who'd get to hold her first. Grandma won.

"*Marhaba!* (hello!), *Sorirart Biro'aitak* (nice to meet you)," Grandma said in a squeaky falsetto.

The comical sound of Mrs. Ibrahim's voice brought smiles to the faces of Momar and Muhammed.

The elated new grandfather stood up and put his hands on the shoulders of the new father.

"So, my son, how, may I ask is the new mother? Tell us about my Sabira."

The somber look in their son-in-law's eyes sandblasted the smiles from their faces and sucked joy from their hearts.

They handed Aneesa back to the nurse, who looked at them with fervent compassion.

Ha-med led them out to the garden. He and his in-laws sat down on a bench. With his arms wrapped around them they shivered and wailed as he told them how brave their Sabira had been. His six feet of youth sheltered their short wide-framed stance.

"While sound in her sleep, she must have been bleeding," Ha-med said. "She awoke looking pale in a pool of fresh blood. Although she was weak, she acted so strong as she whispered to me these words: *Take care of our Aneesa, she is our reason for being, and she is why Allah allowed us to love.*"

To a background of tormented sobs, Ha-med continued.

"She showed me no fear as her gentle hands grasped mine. She was tranquil as she accepted her fate. The doctor asked me to wait outside. As I started to part she stared into my eyes."

Muhammed Hassan turned to Sabira's mother, then father, and whispered their daughter's last words:

"Please shed no tears for me when I have ascended, for the love that we share will forever live on. When you gaze into the eyes of our precious Aneesa, you will know I am watching from heaven above. You and my parents are blessed with Aneesa. Smile my sweet husband. Please do not cry."

The Ibrahims sat there with requiemed faces, quivering. Their voices were clear when they made their request to see Sabira.

They walked into the main lobby and Ha-med phoned the hospital switchboard operator.

"This is Mr. Hassan. I need to speak with Dr. Brennen immediately."

He continued in an urgent tone, "Put me through to her home!"

The operator patched him right through. The phone kept on ringing; Ha-med just kept holding. Time stood still.

Dr. Brennen had arrived at her home twenty minutes before. She plopped down on the couch, too tired to move. The twenty feet from her couch to her bedroom required more vigor than she could spare.

The ringing telephone startled her. As she stretched to grab it, it fell, clattering as it bounced on the hard wooden floor. Composing herself, she answered with a stern, "Hello?"

"This is Muhammed Hassan. I am terribly sorry to bother you. It would mean a great deal to Sabira's parents if they could see their daughter."

Dr. Marjorie Brennen's adrenalin flowed like that fresh cup of coffee after a restful night's sleep.

"Of course. It's no bother at all. I will be right there. Meet me in the main lobby in fifteen minutes."

With gymnast's finesse she slipped out of her scrubs, running to the shower while gargling Scope.

The invigorating, cool water revived her weary body. She dried off and slid into her panties and bra. She fluffed up her shoulder-length layered brown hair then slipped on clean scrubs and a wrinkled white coat. Her feet found their clogs on her way out the door. She jumped into her car that was parked right outside. Ten minutes had passed since she received the call.

Her black Mustang pulled up to the hospital door. As the sliding glass doors of the lobby slid open, the anguished trio stood waiting for her.

"Thank you so much for coming. This is Mr. and Mrs. Ibrahim, Sabira's parents," said Ha-med.

"Please allow me to express my deepest condolences and sincere regret for your terrible loss."

They followed her down a long ominous hallway, which led to a door with a sign that said, "Morgue."

The doctor unlocked the large gray metal door. On a stainless steel table beneath a white sheet was the eerie appearance of a woman's profile. Mr. Ibrahim nodded to say they were ready. She pulled the sheet down to reveal just Sabira's face.

"I will leave you alone now. Please take as much time as you need. I'll be waiting right outside."

With a compassionate nod she walked out of the room, partially closing the door behind her.

Through the door of the cold solid echoing room the prayers they recited were heard in the hall:

"*Inna lil Allahi wa inna ilaihi raaji'un.*"

They walked out and thanked Dr. Brennen for her patience. They escorted her to her car and they thanked her again.

3

The American Dream

Muhammed lay sleeping, his mind wide-awake. His eyes fluttered to and fro.

"How could Allah tease the world, affording it just a glimpse of Sabira … of perfection?" His thoughts echoed. "Was her existence nothing more than a cruel mirage?"

Next to Ha-med, where Sabira had slept, was now only a grief-filled abyss overflowing with pain. The brisk morning sun caused the skeleton trees to shed icicle tears on his suburban home.

Mr. Hassan dragged himself up still clutching the picture he held in his hands when he drifted to sleep. A loose white silk shirt draped the ingénue's body and her iridescent green eyes singed a hole in his heart.

Sabira Ibrahim had been raised in a middle class home, neither extravagant nor lacking in the essentials. Her parents had left Beirut two decades before to start a new life in America. They had arrived in New York and settled in a small Long Island Community. From a lineage of chefs, they came with a skill and opened a restaurant in the center of town. They named it "Mahshi" which in Arabic means *stuffed.*

With little money but conviction to spare, they strived hard and lived the American dream. They bought a small home on the outskirts of town, with trees in the yard and a park down the street. Humble by American standards, it nevertheless surpassed the Ibrahim's wildest dreams.

Mrs. Ibrahim gave birth to an unblemished daughter who struggled to be an "American girl."

For Sabira's sixth birthday they bought her a piano. By twelve she had won many youth competitions and impressed fine pianists older than she. In school she was verbal and knew all the answers. At home she was bound by Islamic restraint.

Sabira became an exquisite young woman with a heavenly face and quick witty charm. When she strolled by, every head would turn. Her self-esteem blossomed along with her breasts. Her parents were strict and forbade her to date; she accepted these terms and stayed sheltered from boys.

She spent her spare time helping her mother at Mahshi's. Her father spent his free time in prayer at the Mosque.

On the first morning of Sabira's sweet sixteenth year, she awoke in the arms of her mother's embrace.

"Your Father and I wish to see you this evening, and present you with a gift that will last your whole life," Mrs. Ibrahim said.

After a pause, she continued to speak with a crack in her voice and a tear in her eye.

"As soon as you get out of school join us at Mahshi's. Help us to close early. This special occasion will not disappoint you. It's a moment you'll cherish the rest of your days."

As Sabira went off to school, her mother waved with a smile, and then blotted her eyes. As the school day progressed, her concentration lagged.

While her eagerness sprinted, the minutes crawled by. She looked at her watch. It was a minute to three.

Like runners on their marks, her anticipation was terminated by the loud clanging bell. She rushed to her locker, loaded her backpack, and flew.

Sabira's feet never touched ground as she ran a mile in near-record time. When she reached the street where their restaurant stood, she glanced at her watch. It was ten minutes past three. Bent over with exhaustion, she placed her hands on her knees. Her heart was racing as she took long, deep breaths.

As Sabira approached the restaurant, she stared and scratched her head. She was bewildered. The shades were pulled down and the building was dark. She unfastened the door and eased herself in. From the darkness within, she heard whispers and rustling.

From out of the darkness lights flashed, music played. Big banners, balloons, and streamers adorned every square inch in a most merry "Happy Birthday" Mardi Gras mood.

Her family's friends packed into the undersized room and served Arabic treats. Hummus-filled bowls emptied as fast as they filled. There was laughter and music, and for the main course spiced lamb and potatoes.

Father and the Imam were armed with papers, a pen and intense expressions as they sat alone in a corner booth. Sabira wondered what could be so important as the two men stood up, shook hands and kissed on the cheeks. The Imam departed. Father returned.

The encore was a festive rice pudding and pastries accompanied by yogurt and scrumptious dried fruits. Some guests sat and talked, others stood up and sang; women told stories while men told bad jokes.

The host said goodnight and Sabira gave thanks as the smiling well-wishers departed. Sabira and her parents locked up and drove home. A thick air of solemnity fogged the front seat renewing Sabira's instinctive concern. The vision of her mother's tears, the faces of her father and the Imam, and now this silent tension.

"You really surprised me with the party. It was such a special evening. I love you both very much."

Sabira hesitated, took a deep breath, and continued.

"Is everything alright?"

"Yes my darling daughter," her mother turned toward her and continued.

"It is difficult to watch you grow up so quickly. And into such a beautiful mature young woman. Where have the years gone?"

They stopped at a red light, and silence prevailed. Mr. Ibrahim looked at his daughter through the rear view mirror.

"Sabira, you have made your mother and I very proud. Allah has been good to us." As the light turned green, he paused, cleared his throat, and continued: "We have a special gift waiting for you at the house."

When they got home there were two boxes on the table. One was small, flat and round. The second was larger and rectangular. They were bound together with a ribbon, a rose and a flask of perfume. Sabira hovered, while her parents anchored themselves on the edge of the couch. Her curiosity quelled her unease. At her mother's request she first took the small box. Inside was a beige satin case with a hinge. As she lifted its lid in slow motion, her eyelids spread wider than ever before; she marveled at its contents. Inside the case was a long thin gold chain. She held it and squinted at its three dangling diamonds.

"I think this necklace is winking at me."

"Come here my daughter and sit on the couch between mother and I."

He placed his hands on his daughter's shoulders.

"Your mother and I present you with this gift in celebration of the most special moment in a young woman's life – the occasion of your engagement to be married."

He kissed her face one cheek at a time. Tears gushed from Sabira's eyes.

Ambushed by her parents, she stood up and began pacing like a defiant soldier. She marched into the kitchen and crashed down on a chair. Head in hands, elbows firm on the thick tabletop. Her father and mother pulled up two more chairs. Sabira stood up, took a step, then faced them and spoke.

"I am barely sixteen. This cannot be happening. We live in America! This is the twentieth century – almost the twenty-first!"

She stared straight and pierced deep into her father's dark eyes. Like a newly polished mirror he returned her harsh gaze.

Sabira's parents, and their parents, and all parents before them had been told whom to marry as well as on what day. They lived, and they loved and their lives became merged. No affairs, no divorces, no "trial separations." No one's broken heart memoirs. Who can argue success?

Sabira could not have prepared for this coming of age, although she had always known it would someday arrive.

She and her father dreaded this moment and the inevitable scene took them both by surprise. Their faces transformed.

Grim stares dissolved into smiles. Sabira wrapped her arms tightly around her father's round body and they bathed one another in showers of tears. It was clear that Sabira accepted her fate. Mother sighed and joined in this emotional circle while blotting both their eyes as well as her own.

"And then, if I may ask, when do I get to meet the mystery man whom you've chosen for me to marry?"

A flat box adorned with a flask of perfume sat on the table. Mrs. Ibrahim lifted it and teased her daughter.

"What lies inside is a treasure indeed. Its value much greater than diamonds and gold." Sabira grabbed it, shook it, held it next to her ear and shook it again.

"What could possibly surpass my necklace of diamonds and gold?"

"Open it slowly and cherish this moment. May Allah bless you and your husband with children."

Meticulously, Sabira's long fingers peeled away the glossy silver wrapping paper that her mother had carefully re-applied after previewing its contents. It housed a shiny black box with a gold label in French that said *Les Beau Dons Par Madeleine* (Fine Gifts by Madeleine).

As she lifted its lid, a weightless sheet of scented tissue paper floated away. Mother and daughter inhaled with eyes closed as Sabira's untarnished youth flushed with a fresh sense of warmth.

Staring at her was the face of a man whom she'd love for the rest of her life. His dark eyes, strong ethnic nose, manicured beard, veneered olive skin, and his slightly parted lips had been created by God to make women's hearts quiver and their fantasies flow.

There was an inscription in the lower right hand corner, "To my dearest Sabira. May Allah guide and protect us as he best sees fit. May our lives coalesce as we two become one. May our love be as vast as the soft desert sands."

It was signed: "Muhammed."

Cupid's arrow pierced her heart as she guarded the photo like an antique plate of glass. She sat back and listened as her mother spoke of her fiancé eight years her senior.

Muhammed Hassan was completing his studies at the Sorbonne. In one year he would receive his Masters of Architecture degree.

At the age of seven, he had been uprooted. He was orphaned during a conflict on the West Bank, which was then part of Jordan.

An old man named Bassan knew Muhammed's father.

Bassan had taken in the young boy as his own, and their hearts and their souls merged like amalgam. Bassan owned a gift shop in the Old Arab Quarter and shared with Muhammed his modest hard-earned pay.

The two of them lived right upstairs. Bassan hired "Ha-med" (as the elder man had come to call him) to help him out after school. By the time he turned twelve, Ha-med could run the whole shop. He could buy and sell and negotiate deals.

On Fridays they'd go to the Dome of the Rock where Ha-med would hear stories and study Koran.

Everyone noticed Ha-med's special gift. He could quiet a mob with an improvised story. The elders admired the crowds he attracted. Children assembled to hear Ha-med's tales. Men came to hear him discuss the Koran and teenage girls gathered to stare at Ha-med.

His charisma attracted locals and tourists who were buying carpets, pottery and regional crafts. Bassan started carrying higher-quality items and shipping these items all over the world. They soon outgrew the old crowded shop and Bassan started dreaming of a better life.

He had a childhood friend who had settled in Haifa. Dr. Shahid Assad was a professor of engineering at Technicon. They had not seen each other in years.

Bassan phoned him and they spoke of their lives, of Ha-med, the shop and of his desire to relocate. Together they began to formulate a plan. On a Thursday, Bassan entrusted the shop to Ha-med, saying he was off to visit some friends.

His quest began. He drove ninety miles to Haifa, met with Assad, and joined his family for dinner that evening at their home in the Sha'anan neighborhood. Assad's wife and son were delighted to meet Bassan after hearing his name for years. After dinner they formulated an enterprising strategy to pursue Bassan's ambition.

The next morning at eight they met with a realtor, Deborah Weiss. Ms. Weiss chauffeured them around in her blue Lincoln Towne Car to scores of locations all over town.

Each was OK, but none was great. Bassan was stunned by the high asking prices but would not let this sway his conviction or dream.

They stopped at a café on a bustling street surrounded by theatres, gift shops and boutiques. Bassan knew that this neighborhood was just what he needed.

He feared that the prices were out of his league. Though discouraged, he would not lose hope. He looked up to Allah and he thought of Ha-med.

They spoke as they ate and watched shoppers stroll by.

Deborah recalled an exclusive new listing. She scrolled down the page. It was two blocks away.

"There's a fabulous place just a short walk from here. It was a cute bookstore called Sabra's. A large bookstore chain opened up down the street. And, so? What else is new? That was the end of Sabra's. Although it is pricey, it couldn't hurt to take a look. No?"

They finished their meal and as they strolled over, Bassan saw the "for sale" sign on a busy street corner.

He froze in his tracks: It was perfect. Love at first sight.

The storefront was on Paris Square next to kiosks and fine shops. They took a look around. It would need no repairs. Only the removal of some bookshelves, building a few showcases and designing a sign. It had an upstairs loft that he could use as an office.

They drove back to Deborah's office. Bassan and Shahid enjoyed Ms. Weiss' performance when she got on the phone.

"Hey Shlomo, I hear you're representing that overpriced shop in Paris Square that needs all that work. I may have found an interested party. Since we know no one has, or will make an offer, we'd hate to see it foreclose. No? So, *nu*? What do you say we help the present owners stop making mortgage payments on it?"

Deborah and Shlomo were cast from the same mold and they'd known each other forever. Two hours of *kibbitzing* calls back and forth included offers, counter-offers, mortgage companies, credit bureaus, banks, lawyers.

And then, a deal was struck. They went to the bank, Assad co-signed the papers and "Bassan's Fine Home Arts" was born.

They went back to Assad's and dined on the veranda. He referred to Haifa as "Heaven on earth" with a quarter of a million people making an effort to get along – churches, synagogues, mosques, shrines and temples all subscribing to The Golden Rule.

After dinner they entered the study, where an entire wall was covered with an aerial photograph of Haifa.

Assad pointed out key sites. A German colony established in 1868, the Golden Domed Baha'i Shrine, the Emit Dahij Foundation promoting religious tolerance, the Stella Maris Church and Carmelite Monastery and the Mahmoud Mosque inside Kababir village.

The more Bassan listened, the more convinced he became.

On Saturday morning they started to organize Bassan's Fine Home Arts. A sign in Arabic, Hebrew and English was ordered for above the large window. Plans were drawn. Designers were hired. Painters and carpenters furnished bids and got to work.

Bassan called Deborah, and they took one more drive – this time in search of the right place to live. With money Bassan had been saving for years, he purchased a small, furnished two-bedroom home.

Bassan drove from Haifa to his crowded shop in the Old City. Ha-med had just finished shipping some rugs.

"Muhammed, make a big 'For Sale' sign for this worn-out place. Then go upstairs and pack up your things," said Bassan.

"Has something happened? What's wrong? Is Israel expecting some trouble?" said Ha-med.

"Nope, not that I know of."

He smiled at Ha-med's fretful expression. The two sat down and went over the details. Ha-med was speechless, a rare site indeed. Bassan's closing sale was an unexpected success with half-off all items and free shipping. With so little left their packing took less than a day. They rented a truck and off they went.

For Ha-med, whose universe had been the Old City, the entrance to Haifa was a breathtaking site.

The sandy beaches and snow-capped mountains pried open his eyes and locked shut his mouth. They drove through the city right up their store. In gold letters on a black background was the trilingual sign, *Bassan's Fine Home Arts.* They worked night and day for two weeks.

They welcomed the town to a Grand Opening celebration. From day one, Bassan's exuded class and charm. One month later, it had clients and contacts. Ha-med and Bassan opened their doors before dawn every day, offering newspapers, coffee and pastries to those passing by.

Passers-by became browsers, browsers became clients, clients referred friends and the business took off. They sold carpets, lighting accessories, and embellishments to brighten the workplace and home.

Several years passed.

They started carrying custom-made furniture, and expanded to include a gallery with artwork on consignment. Their reputation spread. They began to assist designers in furnishing homes. Bassan gracefully aged. He began spending less time at the shop and more time at rest. Ha-med's spent his days running the shop, and his nights caring for his aging mentor.

One Sunday morning, a middle-aged couple was strolling and stopped just to browse.

Yoav Goldstein had been born in Haifa. He had pursued his studies at Columbia Law. While in New York he'd met and married Shaina, an interior designer with a master's degree.

She had grown up in the sixties with flowers and peace. Yoav had fought for the Army in Israel back then. Shaina's laissez-faire spirit and Yoav's conservative ways stuck together like Velcro. Once they were married, they returned to Haifa. She designed from their home while Yoav practiced law.

This happenstance meeting of Ha-med and the Goldsteins produced a lifelong friendship. Shaina accepted a position as interior design consultant at Bassan's Fine Home Arts. She told Ha-med stories of life in New York, and the teenage romantic would fall asleep gazing at photographs of the City. He would dream of the culture, imagine the lights; yet he knew that these visions were just dusk till dawn.

Ha-med's first two decades of life flew by. These same years for Bassan ebbed and flowed like the tides. In a transition as smooth as green leaves turn golden-brown, his century approached and his health declined. His once thick hair was now sparse and his speech sometimes slurred, his quick wit had slowed and his vision was blurred.

One cool summer evening, a north wind blew past. It whispered that this night was to be his last. The ocean's fresh scent oozed into Bassan's room, lit by one bright star and a crescent-shaped moon. This kind good-willed man held his head way up high, though its weight on his shoulders now tired him out. His body was tranquil. His mind was content. His soul was prepared.

His Ha-med was not.

Ha-med looked into the eyes of the only father he had ever known, and wept. He struggled to speak of the good times they had: the old shop, the new shop, the fun, the success. Bassan forced a smile, stretched for a tissue and dabbed Ha-med's eyes. He then placed his thin hand over Ha-med's mouth and whispered, "Shhh."

He placed his palms on Ha-med's cheeks, looked up to the heavens, and spoke.

"We are merely visitors here, just passing through. Allah blessed me with a visit from you in the evening of my life."

He paused, sighed and closed his eyes. Ha-med's torn emotions bounced from nervous sniffling chuckles to trembling sobs.

"Ha-med, your prayers to Allah shall always be answered, though you may be surprised by the answers received. Struggle to search for the answers you need. Be content with your lot, be wary of greed. I leave you in God's almighty hands. May He grant you the ability to contribute good things to the world and the capacity to find joy in all things that you do."

Ha-med placed his head on Bassan's old frail chest and listened to his muffled heartbeat fade and then cease.

A typhoon of grief swept over him. Ha-med's wailing was thunder, his tears: a monsoon. His sorrow was like lightning. It stormed for three days.

4

Bon Voyage

Ha-med buried Bassan, and closed the shop for three days. Bassan's home, his shop, his employees, his income and his responsibilities were now in Ha-med's capable hands.

His choreographed mornings were precise and routine. At sunrise he'd shower, put on the coffee, fetch the paper and peruse it over breakfast. He'd then drive over to Bassan's, enter through the rear door, switch on the lights, check the displays, grab some cash from the safe, fill the register, unlock the front door, pop up the window shade, flip the sign to "open" and finally grab some tables and chairs and set them outside.

When Shaina arrived they went over their projects and contracts. Shaina's keen insight into New York's trendy fads contrasted with Ha-med's down to earth mid-east approach.

Their unique complement forged a style that quickly caught on. Their catalogue was a hit on the biggest shopping stage of them all – New York City!

One day, a "high-maintenance" couple strolled in, looked around and was impressed to no end. They had recently purchased an outstanding property upon which they planned to build their dream house.

Already having assembled a team of designers, engineers, and architects, they invited Bassan's Fine Home Art*s* to join the team.

The next morning at sunrise Ha-med walked the lot, took photographs, and brainstormed with Shaina. The goal: design a unique home to embellish the landscape, make a statement and provide unhindered views of the mountains and sea. The schedule called for a preliminary drawing in three months.

While the architects arranged upcoming weeks and hurriedly completed prior commitments, Ha-med wasted no time. He got right on it, spending evenings and weekends at the university immersed in architectural designs. He envisioned a concept and started to sketch.

Ha-med's office floor swore to his determination. Soon there was no room to walk without crunching. Rejected drawings formed wall-to-wall mountains of tightly crumpled sketch paper balls. On Friday he paroled himself down to an art store, and sacks of supplies escorted him back. On Monday he was pardoned with a drawing and model.

This two-story, steel structure's immense thick glass walls merged with towering stone slabs. Flowing water mimicked the ocean's waves. A rough stucco finish admired the mountains and engulfed the terrain.

He sold his concept. An architect took over. The builders knew this one was Ha-med's design.

Ha-med treasured each aspect of building construction from concept to groundbreaking; foundation to roof. Talented architects noticed this novice. They respected his input and used his ideas. He had long daydreamed of life as an architect. When thoughts of enrolling at night crossed his mind, guilt thwarted their path. How could he not be satisfied with his life? How dare he for a moment forget the hideous plight from which he had narrowly escaped? Why had his life been spared?

That night as he drifted off to sleep, he felt his body tremble and the ground rumble. He tried to awaken but could not. He envisioned the horrific life he once lived, watching as others around him were slaughtered or worse. Many survived ... void of limbs, void of eyes, void of souls.

Orphans grew up starving, malnourished, in impoverished conditions. Never aware of the truth; knowing not who to blame. Their leaders rule high from their palatial mountains while their subjects live low in their shadows in filth. Why not use riches for clinics and schools? Instead they build factories, which churn out grenades that they strap to the backs of their children in hate.

As his nightmares give way to his alarm clock's soft music, Ha-med vividly pictures his sister's smiling face, her cute pudgy lips and magnificent eyes.

Then an explosion rips her apart – splattered like road-kill all over the thick adobe walls of their quaint West Bank home.

Ha-med awoke in a panic, heart racing, struggling to breath, drenched with sweat. He recalled once again that his life had been spared, and his daily routine started over again. He headed off to work.

He came to work tired, with a textbook in hand and an *Architectural Digest* displayed on his desk. Shaina arrived with a cheerful "Good morning!" but saw in his eyes that he had not slept well. She sensed his frustration and shared his regrets. They reviewed contracts, met clients, and made sales all day. Shaina's day sprinted while Ha-med's crawled by.

As they locked up, Shaina said, "Hey, Ha-med. Got any plans? "

"Yeah, I'm running late. The Prime Minister is meeting with me, President Bush and Yassar Arafat for cookies and ice cream at my place."

"Real cute. Ya wanna check out the Hashmi-Barnavon Home? The painters are finishing their touch-ups. They're closing on it next week."

"Sure," Ha-med said. He followed her over.

They had worked closely with the architect on this one for over a year. They proudly strolled around and admired their work. Its' grand entranceway had twin spiral staircases leading to a cantilevered landing. As Shaina was heading out the door she peeked around a limestone column and caught a glimpse of Ha-med atop the landing. The crystal chandelier was dim in contrast to his euphoric grin. His hands were at ease on the wrought iron rail as he turned towards the window and prayed. Shaina revered seeing Ha-med so proud. They walked out together and bid each other good night. She called Yoav from her car.

"Hi honey. Sorry. I'm running late. I'll explain when I'm home. Love ya, see ya soon." Before Yoav spoke, he heard a *click*. He entered the study and sprawled himself out on the couch. Twenty minutes later she walked through the door, gave him a kiss and sat down with her knees bent, her shoes off, her feet on the table and her hands locked around her legs. They asked each other how their days were, and they were fine.

"I think Ha-med would make a superb architect," said Shaina, out of nowhere. "He just has this knack, it's in his blood."

"And what does our Ha-med think of *your* idea?"

"Well sweetie, we've both been so busy lately. We've not had the time to discuss it in detail."

"Well, my little Shai-na-la, have you discussed it *at all*?"

Yoav relished in Shaina's *guess what I'm thinking* games. He knew from the start what she was getting at, but was having fun going along for the ride. When he teased her enough he said: "Well, Honey, I agree, Ha-med would most certainly make a superb architect indeed."

So they conspired an irresistible plan, always with Ha-med's best interest in mind. Like a loving aunt and uncle to a struggling young nephew, they derived pleasure from this chance to better his life. For months they made phone calls and gathered information in pursuit of Architectural Schools. As the plan gained momentum and details amassed, it became time to sit down with Ha-med. As Ha-med's birthday approached, Shaina had an idea.

One Monday at lunchtime, as if he was just browsing, Yoav stopped by *Bassan's* for a nosh. Shaina was "just too busy" to even stop and talk, so Ha-med sat down and joined him.

"So, What's this I hear?" said Yoav. "Next Sunday's your birthday?"

"Yep, sure is. Two decades of life. I guess that's not bad?"

"You don't sound terribly excited about the occasion." They sipped thick black coffee from small baked clay cups.

"I know my life's good. I praise Allah each day. I've just never been too excited about birthdays. To me, they're just like any other day."

"Now let's see, what can we do to enhance your excitement?" Yoav took another sip of coffee, and continued, " Well, how 'bout we take a trip? I need to go to France next week. Would you like to come?"

"I'd love to, but next week? Got deadlines, appointments, you know. And with you and Shaina out, who'd watch the shop? How 'bout a rain-check?"

"Would you *really* like to go some time?"

"*Does the bear ... Is the Pope ...* Oh, never mind. I really would!"

"Happy Birthday. We've made the arrangements. Shaina will stay and take care of the shop. Your employees all know you'll be gone for five days."

His jaw fell open and his eyes widened. When he was able to speak he asked when they would leave.

"Go home and get packed. Our flight's in two days, Wednesday at ten, I'll pick you up at six." Yoav stood up, smiled and strutted off proudly as Ha-med went back inside to whispers, giggles – and a banner of the Eiffel Tower with the words: "Bon Voyage" printed across it.

Shaina gave Ha-med a big kiss on the cheek and her red lipstick blended right in. "Happy Birthday, go see an eyeful of towering sights," said Shaina. When his blush subsided, he spoke in a comically serious tone. "OK break time is over. Clock out or get back to work."

Two mornings later the Goldsteins relaxed over coffee and bagels. Then Shaina kissed Yoav, told him to have a great trip and handed him a package to give to Ha-med.

Yoav drove over to find Ha-med waiting outside like a kid on his first day of summer camp. He was primed, raring to go. Ben Gurion Airport was sixty miles away. They took a leisurely drive and when they arrived at the airport, they checked in, sat down on a bench, kicked up their feet and took in the sights.

Ha-med and Yoav were experienced in the fine art of people watching, and the ethnic collage was an observers dream: Arabs in black turbans and robes, Jews with black hats and beards, a Western teen with crutches and skis, Middle Eastern women revealing only their eyes entertained by a loud group of nuns. There were babbling tongues amongst bald silent monks and ladies with scarves on their heads. Men with small caps, a few red, many black. Young children running and laughing amidst soldiers with stern looks and guns.

"Ha-med? So, what do you think," said Yoav, as he leaned over and asked rhetorically: "Is life a miracle, or what?"

"Ya know what Einstein said?" asked Ha-med.

"I believe Einstein said lots of things, didn't he?" said Yoav.

"There are two ways to look at life" said Ha-med. "As though *nothing* is a miracle, or as though *everything* is a miracle."

A crackling, distorted announcement reverberated overhead. "El Al flight 323 from Tel Aviv to Paris will now begin boarding. Passengers please proceed to the gate."

This was Ha-med's first flight. Nervously he took the window seat, braced himself for the worst, and grabbed the armrests while gazing out the window. The takeoff was smooth and Ha-med was relieved. When they reached cruising altitude Yoav shrugged his shoulders while handing over Shaina's package with a smile. Ha-med opened it, and found two books. One was a leather bound hand colored Koran with parchment-like pages and fine gold leaf edging. It was a reproduction of an ancient work that was said to be the oldest in existence. Only two of the originals remained. The second book was an enormous *Architectural Atlas of the World.* Inside it was an inscription, and a riddle.

"Ha-med, Go out and build us a New World. What does a man who suffers from arthritis have in common with your trip to Paris?" Yoav smirked but kept quiet not to spoil the fun. As they got closer to France Yoav picked up the atlas.

"So, Ha-med, what do you think? Wanna be an Architect some day?"

"Some day, sure. In my next life. Perhaps Allah needs some help renovating his heavenly palace?"

"Have you some pressing engagements in this life?"

"Yeah, right," said Ha-med.

"Seriously, think about it," said Yoav.

"C'mon Yoav. That requires college, graduate school, brains. Besides, I owe it to Bassan to keep the business going. It's my way of keeping him alive."

"Well, let's see. Brains, you've got. College? Graduate school? All you need for that is brains. And those, you've got. And what would Bassan want anyway? Think about it. Shaina and I could lease your property, and run your business while you're in school. Bassan's legacy would continue uninterrupted. Your cake, and eat it too! Anyway, just a thought."

As the plane's landing gear descended, Ha-med's gears shifted into overdrive. "Please fasten your seatbelts, place tray tables and seat backs in the full upright position."

Deplaning, they headed through customs and on their way to the baggage claim, Ha-med saw a slight man with an enormous sign that said: "Muhammed Hassan, Welcome to Paris. Enjoy your tour of the Sorbonne School of Architecture."

Yoav had been in contact with a professor of Architecture at the Sorbonne and told him all about Ha-med. Architects from Haifa provided glowing recommendations.

Ha-med's gleeful child-like reaction was deeply etched in Yoav's mind. Ha-med hugged Yoav just short of making a scene.

"Oh, I get it," said Ha-med, "an arthritic has a *sore bone.* Very funny."

He toured the Sorbonne, filled out applications, met with professors and sat in on a class. They ran around Paris, then headed back home, sat down and made plans. They leased an apartment and Ha-med enrolled for the following year. The Goldsteins had made Ha-med an outstanding business proposition. Off went the student to study in France.

Ha-med immersed himself in his studies. He was as enthusiastic and devoted as a student could be. Outspoken in class, he always sat right upfront, but outside of classes he kept to himself. Most found it strange that this handsome young man preferred solitude to parties, movies to bars. Ha-med liked outdoor concerts, and gallery hopping. He joined the Islamic Center, and attended the Mosque.

On the student activities board, a poster said: "Emit Dahij, PhD to speak on Monotheism: Brotherhood under our one common God." Dr. Dahij's foundation was based in Haifa. His philosophy was Gandhi-esque; *peaceful* resistance can defeat guns and bombs and "love thy neighbor."

Dr. Dahij had spent a few years of his studies in Boston when Dr. Timothy Leary had been popular on the west coast. His message was boring and cliché to many but Ha-med enjoyed his smooth style and words.

This professor was tall, neat and clean-shaven. He had dark beady eyes, and wore small reading glasses on the bridge of his long drooping nose. Although not handsome by any account, his soft-spoken style eclipsed his odd looks. In his left hand, he always carried his sacred Koran after which Ha-med's reproduction was fashioned.

After the lecture, Ha-med introduced himself. They spoke of Haifa, and of their common philosophy. They shook hands and parted, not knowing that fate would some day have their paths cross again.

After two months in Paris, Ha-med became afflicted with the highly contagious French bicycling bug. He relentlessly shopped until he found a cure. Saturday mornings were his times to cruise and he'd do so without boredom, without a care in the world. He would tackle high inclines, and then dream his way down. One such Saturday after he finished exploring new sites he sat beneath a tree, propped-up his bike, leaned back and admired the magnificence of the tree's far-reaching tributary-like branches breaking the magnificent sky into hundreds of abstract, still-life geometric designs. Across from the park was a Synagogue with a group of young adults mingling out front. One of Ha-med's classmates noticed him. She was a lovely girl, blue eyes and brown hair, in a stylish skirt an awfully tight sweater.

"Hey Ha-med!" yelled Michelle from across the street. "Whatcha' doin'?"

"Hey, Michelle. Relaxing. Taking in the sights."

"It's so nice to see you with your head in the clouds, and not in your books."

She and some friends went over to chat. They were going for a nosh, and Ha-med walked along with his bicycle and joined them. While solving the world's problems and matching wits over croissants and iced tea, two of their classmates flashed by the window. Ha-med had also known them from the mosque. He stood up to greet them, squinting from the sun's blinding glare through the window, but they were already gone.

The conversation resumed, and the day passed. They split the bill and walked out together to find a disheartening site. Where Ha-med's bicycle had been now lay a twisted pile of bent metal, shredded rubber, and a note on the slashed leather seat: "To the Jew-loving traitor."

To Ha-med's new friends, it was just a bad moment. Temporary.

But to Ha-med, it was much worse. He could not comprehend what would drive someone to this.

The group asked around but no one had seen anything. How could this have happened without anyone noticing, on a crowded Paris street on a Saturday afternoon?

He said goodbye to Michelle and his new friends and although they were not to blame, they felt guilty nonetheless. As Ha-med stared down on the heap of twisted anger, he reflected on his past, and pondered his future. A future whose intricacies and challenges reached far beyond his most vivid imagination and wildest dreams.

5

Unconditional Love

Muhammed Hassan finished his Masters, graduated with honors, married Sabira and accepted a position at a prestigious New York City architectural firm. The Goldstein's leased his property in Haifa, rented out his home, and Shaina took over Bassan's Fine Home Arts. Sabira and Ha-med bought a home on Long Island not far from her parents.

Ha-med and Sabira shared an unending love while they desperately tried to ignore their one flaw: Her womb remained barren in spite of their prayers. To comfort each other they downplayed their dismay though in solitary moments, each wept.

One night Ha-med worked past midnight; Sabira felt ill, so he let her just sleep. That next quiet morning the sun nudged Ha-med and he stretched and admired his magnificent wife.

Oblivious she dosed, her breasts rising and falling as their silhouette beamed through a fine veil of silk. The sun glanced at her breasts through the cracks in the blinds and they countered the sun with a radiant glow.

Ha-med leaned over and kissed her soft neck; she pretended to sleep to prolong this caress. As his face brushed her jaw his beard tickled her neck. She opened her eyes, and with untamed emotion, she burst into tears.

"Our prayers have been answered!" While blotting her eyes, she continued, "Allah planted a seed. Our child now grows."

Ha-med's hands rubbed her back as he then wiped her tears. He was overwhelmed, speechless.

His eyes said it all. Stuttering and fumbling he asked, "When?"

She lifted her shirt to display her cute belly, "February the fourth, if the Doctor's correct."

Sabira sat up on the edge of the bed and Ha-med stood, kissed her lips, and kneeled before her. She dangled her legs trapping him in between. His feather soft lips headed south past her breasts and he paused at her belly and gave it a kiss. Her arms wrapped around him; their hearts pounded, tears flowed. He eased her on to her back as his passion engorged.

"Sabira, please ... Don't move a muscle. Stay just as you are." Ha-med jumped up, snapped the blinds shut, grabbed the phone and called work.

"McDaniel and Stoltz. Brenda speaking. How may I help you have a beautiful day?"

Brenda had an erotic voice, incongruous with her well-nourished appearance.

Four wealthy ex-husbands supported her habits. Fake nails and eyelashes re-done once a week. Despite her love-failings, Brenda was a warm sensitive woman who every one loved. Her 25 years at the firm gave her influence in the office and clout with the boss.

"Good morning Brenda," said Ha-med with a sigh of relief. "Something personal has come up."

Sabira giggled as Ha-med continued, "Would you please ask Mr. Stoltz if I could take the day off?"

"Mr. Hassan, is everything alright? You sound a bit winded, out of breath. Anything I could do?"

"No Brenda. Thanks. Everything's terrific!" His wife giggled again. "What I mean is ... it would be great if the boss had no deadlines or models he needed finished today." He shook his head toward Sabira, and she grinned as she covered her mouth.

"Jus' take the day off, Hon. I'll deal with the boss. You two go have some fun."

Sabira was glowing; legs still dangling, breasts and belly exposed. He kneeled down before her, parting her legs again.

His lips and tongue tickled her thighs. She grabbed his thick hair to restrain his intentions attempting to quell his desire to please.

After a struggle, her body surrendered and she stroked Ha-med's scalp and massaged his broad back. His mouth's gentle rhythm brought her to the verge. With her rapture approaching, his head pulled away, and he held her in fear that she might be a dream. The tip of his tongue on her now pregnant breasts made her aroused nipples firmer than sun-ripened grapes. His engorgement plunged into her sweltering core. He thrusted, retreated and thrusted again as his lips' forceful suction grabbed onto her breasts; his hands squeezed her muscular gyrating buttocks, and she gasped to the echoing cries of her name.

She toppled him over and her lean petite body had Ha-med's pinned down. She slowed to delay his ecstatic eruption. Her hands grabbed his chest, her back arched, her motions quickened. Her erotic cave was a pulsating vice. His body filled hers with thick climactic warmth as she vigorously milked him to the crescendos of moans.

As one, they slept in the warmth of their bodies while the day passed. The sun set and the moon smiled on them.

They awoke to the evening's refreshing cool air. Together they showered and put on their robes. They spoke of a meal, but dared not leave the house. They strolled to the bedroom and found it in shambles. He smiled. She blushed. As Sabira was changing the blankets and sheets, Ha-med said he'd go make them something to eat.

He sculpted a luscious fruit salad. He returned and Sabira was prone on the bed with her knees gently flexed and her head propped up high. Ha-med sat beside her and hand-fed his Queen. Licking her lips while her eyelashes fluttered she said: "Muhammed, tell me again about the first time you decided to visit New York." Like a child pleading to hear her favorite bedtime story just one more time, she begged, "Oh, please?" She never grew tired of hearing it. He never grew tired of telling it.

"About a decade ago," said Ha-med, "I was standing in line at the jam-packed Paris Airport ticket counter."

His boarding pass was issued. Elbow to elbow he pushed his way through the crowds. He paced, paused, glanced at his watch, and paced again. His dreams of New York were about to be realized. This dream-turned-reality materialized during the previous spring break when the Goldstein's visited him in Paris. As they enthusiastically described New

York's culture, diversity, and unparalleled excitement, Ha-med's curiosity was sparked; he had to see it for himself. They helped arrange an interview with the prestigious New York Architectural firm of McDaniel and Stoltz.

Anxiously awaiting his journey, his days slowed and school dragged. He crossed off each passing day on his calendar. One afternoon after class he peddled home and found a "Photos: DO NOT BEND" parcel waiting on his doorstep. He took it inside and sat on the couch. He stood up, contemplated, scratched his head, and sat down at his desk. He peeled back the edge, reached inside and removed two sheets of fine parchment. Sandwiched between them was an eight inch by ten inch satin-finished photo of a muse. He was mesmerized. Black hair, green eyes, timeless, ageless, flawless. He propped up the picture, and read the letter.

My Dear Mr. Muhammed Hassan,

I am Habib. I recently visited Israel for the first time in decades. In Haifa I looked up and froze. A prophetic sign bearing the name Bassan stood staring at me. I inquired within. Shaina Goldstein spoke so fondly of you.

Bassan and I were the dearest of friends. We also had a common friend named Ibrahim. In our youth, we three were like brothers. I moved away, the Ibrahim's dispersed. We lost contact for decades. The Ibrahim's youngest son and his bride chose a life in New York. When Bassan ascended, his whispers washed up on their steps. Their daughter Sabira, the granddaughter of Bassan's dearest friend, is untarnished. Her beauty and poise will tempt many. As she approaches sixteen, her parents seek a man worthy to know her.

Our time here on earth is but a moment; a fleeting dream. Open your mind and consider my words. I spoke of you to the parents of Sabira. They offer the hand of their daughter to you.

In the words of our Prophet Muhammed (peace be upon him):

"Shall I inform you about the best treasure a man can hoard?

It is a virtuous wife who pleases him whenever he looks towards her."

I remain in his humble service,
Habib

Ha-med's impulses persuaded a rapid decision. He stared at the photograph of Sabira with passionate zeal.

Her luminescence was Cupid's arrow; the mythical archer had scored a direct hit. He sprinted down the street to "Fine Gifts by Madeleine." This upscale shop housed a portrait studio with a tall, thin, soft-spoken photographer sporting a pencil-thin moustache and pungent cologne. Ha-med paid him to rush. He posed him on the chair and positioned the lights.

"Monsieur, please don't smile so much."

Ha-med tried to abide but failed miserably. His grinning lips were stuck. When the shoot was completed he browsed for a frame, and in less than an hour he looked at the photo, inscribed it with words of love and shipped the portrait of himself to New York.

An eager reply followed, but not from his fiancée. Her parents had intercepted his portrait. They opened it, admired it, and rewrapped it. They then made arrangements for Muhammed Hassan to meet their daughter. During Sabira's spring break, Ha-med journeyed to New York to meet his fiancée and interview with McDaniel and Stoltz.

6

Sabira

Ha-med was on his way. When he had first booked his flight he dreamt of his interview, and prayed for a job with McDaniel and Stoltz. And yet these unrealized dreams seemed dwarfed as he clutched Sabira's photograph. His head rested on the airplane's window bobbing and buzzing to the engines vibrations.

"Good afternoon. This is the Captain speaking. The time is seventeen minutes past five and the temperature on the ground is a warm eighty-seven degrees beneath clear blue skies with a gentle breeze out of the north. If you look to your left, you can catch your first glimpse of New York City as we begin our descent."

The sun's blinding rays peaked beneath the small shade. Ha-med snapped it up and out of the way. He was awestruck. The world below made his mind spin. Massive geometric structures of century-old limestone and shimmering glass stood proudly on concrete carpets surrounded by oceans; divided by streams. A never-ending network of titanic steel cables stretched from landmass to landmass, propelling vigorous multitudes in every direction. Mammoth steel centipedes vanished into subterranean tunnels, transporting commuters from workplace to home. And in the midst of the asphalt, antennas, and smog, sat an immense, calm, green lawn with a vast patch of blue.

"Please fasten your seatbelts and place your tray tables and seatbacks in their full upright position. Flight attendants, prepare for landing."

Ha-med grabbed the armrests, bracing himself while still peering out the window in disbelief. The sudden screeching of deceleration told Muhammed Hassan he was in New York City.

"Please stay in your seats, with seatbelts completely fastened until the captain has turned off the fasten-seatbelt sign."

As tends to be the case in New York, the flight attendant's request was ignored by all. By all except Ha-med. He sat mesmerized – frozen, still gazing out the window. When he did disembark, his head twisted and spun like a cyclone of energy as he negotiated the erratic currents that dragged him along. He set anchor at the Immigration desk and a uniformed man spoke through the thick glass.

"May I please see your passport?"

After checking the passport, the man spoke again.

"Muhammed Hassan, you are from Israel, I see. Yet you flew in to New York from France? Please clarify this, and is the nature of your trip business or pleasure?"

Ha-med's mind was still fixed on the breathtaking skyline, vibrant activity and intriguing crowds. The agent had caught him off guard, two questions in one breathe: business or pleasure? Israel or France?

"Well sir, at first it was business that motivated my visit, a job interview, McDaniel and Stoltz, y'know? The architectural firm? … I am from Haifa but I presently attend the Sorbonne … that's in France, so, I am a student in Paris, but Israel is my home ... though technically I was born in Jordan. When I complete my education I think I may move to New York."

Ha-med came up for air, then continued.

"In addition to the business nature of my visit, I also have come for pleasure. I hope to visit many attractions, museums … shows, and, oh, yes, the movies, particularly action/adventure. I also will be meeting a young woman named Sabira who I plan to marry, although … "

The agent cut him off mid-sentence while stamping his passport.

"Enjoy yourself, see lots of things, have a good time."

He was on his way. He was relieved when he saw the sign that said "Men." He rushed in and strolled out. Refreshed and invigorated, he confronted the chaotic mobs swarming in every direction. Muhammed's height helped him peer over the crowds as a sparkling beacon cut through the fog.

Their eyes met.

She was even more exquisite than her photograph.

Young heat-seeking missiles had locked on their targets, ready to burst into passionate flames. He was more handsome than she ever imagined. They approached in slow motion, bound in a trance.

"This is the moment of my dreams. Angels whispered your name while I slept," said Ha-med.

"When slumber descended I called out your name. Allah assured me our lives would soon merge," said Sabira.

Ha-med looked into her parents' glassy eyes.

"I seek your permission and blessing." He paused, and could feel her heart tremble as he held her hands. He knelt before her, one knee on the ground. He again looked towards her parents.

"I request your blessing. May I take your daughter to love as my wife?"

The Ibrahims held hands. With tears in their eyes, they looked at each other. Momar nodded a smile of approval. The four found themselves oblivious to their environment, lost in a dream. Then they looked up.

The plaza, escalators, and overhead platform were packed with a dynamic audience of traveling hordes. Like a dam giving way, a murmuring hush of teary-eyed on-lookers burst out with encouraging cheers and a standing ovation.

With his bag in his left hand, and Sabira's left hand in his right, they followed her parents to the parking garage, boarded the blue four-door Buick sedan and drove out to Long Island. Ha-med and Sabira sat quietly in the back while her parents did most of the talking.

"Your flight was quite long, are you tired? Or hungry? Would you like to have something to eat?" said Mrs. Ibrahim.

"Babi, he's probably tired," said Mr. Ibrahim. "Maybe we should let him unpack and relax?"

"Perhaps we should stop for a snack?"

"Maybe he first wants to freshen up?"

"It's a long drive. Should we stop along the way?"

Sabira and Muhammed sat smiling, gazing, holding hands. "Muhammed," said Sabira, making sure her parents heard her loud and clear. "What would *you* like to do?" said Sabira.

"Well … Let's go to your home. I'll get unpacked and freshen up.

Then let's all get something to eat!"

Sabira just smiled and her parents smiled back. She could tell that they loved him already. They pulled off the highway, and drove for a mile to a delightful suburb on the outskirts of town. They turned down a picturesque tree-lined street, then into the driveway of their two-bedroom home. The detached garage had a stairway that led to a guest room above.

"Welcome to our home. It is now your home too. I think everything you need is upstairs. Clean sheets and blankets, towels, empty drawers, a closet and of course a nice shower. Our kitchen is your kitchen. Open twenty-four hours a day," said Mrs. Ibrahim.

Mr. Ibrahim handed his new friend two keys, one to the guest quarters and one to their home. "With these keys, I hand you my trust."

Ha-med and Sabira just smiled at each other as Ha-med took his bag and headed upstairs. "I shall be down in one hour."

The Ibrahims grinned their way through the front door and Sabira illuminated the room. They teamed up to prepare their new friend a feast. Dad set the table. The girls went to the kitchen and took out some lamb that they sautéed then simmered in a covered clay pot. As Babi continued to prepare the side dishes she looked her glowing love-struck daughter up and down and swooshed her away with the back of her hand.

"Go my princess. Prepare yourself. Get yourself ready for dinner."

Sabira went to her room, slipped out of her clothing and admired herself in the mirror. She made up her face, brushed her hair, and spritzed on a splash of perfume. She made sure her door was shut tight, then opened the bottom drawer of her dresser. Concealed beneath sweaters was a small glossy black bag about the size of a purse. A few days ago while cruising the mall, she felt the warm winds of bravery wisp her along.

She'd ducked into Victoria's Secret. She had no idea. Like a child's first toy store, it was a new world.

"First time in our store, hon?" asked a tall, thin and well-endowed salesgirl.

"Yes M'aam."

"Well, let's see what we need, shall we?"

They went to a fitting room, took some measurements, and selected a few items to try on. The attention she got for the body God gave her made her cheeks blush and hormones soar. Detecting a sense of embarrassment, a customer around forty said: "Darlin', they had you in mind when they designed this stuff."

From Victoria Secret, she went to BeBe and then to Express.

Back in her bedroom, she sat by her mirror on a small tufted soft padded vanity seat. In slow motion she slipped into her thong then positioned her breasts in a sexy new bra. A tingling sensation took her by surprise.

A warm dessert breeze blew throughout her from within. She squeezed into a side-split gray skirt and draped her torso in a slinky black sweater with a shoulder exposed. The finishing touch was her engagement necklace.

She heard the door chime, then looked up and thanked Allah.

Mr. and Mrs. Ibrahim greeted their guest with *Assalaam alaikum,* and Ha-med answered, *Waalaikum Assalaam.*

His nose caught the scent of an Arabic feast. He looked up, closed his eyes and inhaled.

"Have I just entered Allah's kitchen?"

"Give me ten more minutes," Mrs. Ibrahim said. "You two go and relax. I will gather Sabira and we'll call you when dinner is served."

The fiancée and father sat down in his study. Mother returned to the kitchen. Sabira tiptoed behind her and placed her hands over her eyes.

"Guess who?"

"An angel, I'd guess." She turned around and saw her daughter.

"Who are you, and what have you done with my child?"

Posing, then pausing, Sabira said, "Well Mother, what do you think? How do I look?"

"I think in my life I have not seen a more beautiful sight. Your Muhammed will be pleased." She and Sabira sat down, and Mrs. Ibrahim continued. "Your beauty is a powerful gift. Conceal it. Let it not please the eyes nor tempt the minds of other men. Share it only with Muhammed." She paused, smiled, and kissed her daughter's cheeks.

They put the finishing touches on the table. "Now, run off and gather the men for dinner."

The men sat and chatted, told jokes and laughed. Then an angel descended upon them. They jumped to their feet and froze. Their wide-open mouths were without words. Sabira broke the silence.

"C'mon guys, let's go get some food."

During the meal, their pasts were divulged and their future was planned. By the time dessert was served Ha-med was part of the family.

The next morning was the start of new lives for Sabira and Ha-med. The pair set their adrenalin pumps on overdrive, and took off. On the first day they dined in an outdoor café where they sat on a love seat with no room to spare. Sabira described in detail the scene at her home when she received the necklace and photograph. As she spoke, she caught Ha-med in a trance of admiration. She then did something he immediately learned to love. She contracted the muscles between her eyebrows, forcing wrinkles on her wrinkle-free forehead, and causing her eyebrows to furrow and drop.

She scrunched her mouth and nose.

"Whaaat?" she said in a sing-songy voice.

If he looked in her eyes and admired her beauty she would do this maneuver the same every time.

He and Sabira spoke of spending the summer together in France. She knew that her parents would never approve. She looked into his eyes and he took hold of her hands. His face approached hers; her face approached his and their lips eagerly met halfway. Mouths melted, tongues tangled, fantasies flowed.

With their first kiss out of the way, they traversed the entire city holding hands and embracing at every opportunity. Exhausted after a perfect day, they headed back home on the train. The Long Island Railroad stopped three blocks from Mahshi's. The Ibrahims were there and the Imam came by. After they dined, Mrs. Ibrahim said: "It's getting late. Sabira and I will now retire and leave you men alone."

The men stood up, and Ha-med grasped Sabira's hands. "Get a restful night's sleep, we leave at ten in the morning." She and her mother headed home.

The Imam said to Ha-med, "My most sincere congratulations. I have watched Sabira's transformation from child to woman. As a good Muslim man you have many obligations. Among them, to protect your woman, and be wary of others, of non-believers. Stick close to our flock under Allah's protection, or stray and face Allah's harsh wrath."

Puzzled, Ha-med was soft spoken as he requested clarification, "Is there not but one God, the God of Abraham, and Jesus, and our Prophet Muhammed?"

"Yes, why of course, as the Koran has dictated. He is Allah, the One Almighty God of all things!"

"So then, Imam, if an unrighteous non-believer, though a Muslim by birth, lives in sin, disobeying the words of The Prophet? Is he not still a Muslim? Or is he cast out?"

The Imam answered quickly and directly. "As long as one breathes, he has time to repent, to learn, to transform. You, as a good Muslim, have a responsibility ... an obligation, to befriend him and help him to see the right way."

"And Imam, if he is befriended by one who is righteous? One whose footsteps are worthy, whose lips whisper words of compassion and whose deeds are examples of benevolence." Ha-med paused, scratched his chin, and continued, "If the sinner sees the way and transforms, what will become of *the righteous one*?"

"Allah will praise him on earth and reward him in paradise."

"But, Imam, what if this righteous one is a Christian or Jew?"

The Imam, momentarily at a loss of words stood up.

"I will see you for Jumu'ah at the mosque on Friday."

Ha-med and Sabira woke up bright and early and spent another adventurous day strolling hand-in-hand around town. They braved New York's subways so they would not miss a thing.

As the sun began setting, they hailed a taxi and cruised up to the theatre district. They had reservations for dinner at a plush Times Square club owned by McDaniel and Stoltz. As guests of the owners, Ha-med and Sabira passed through the line to the muffles of whispering rumors and stares.

"Who's that fine looking couple?"

"Isn't she *that* model?"

"Isn't that what's his name ... you know ... from ... "

The charming young couple just played right along. They dined, danced and laughed until closing time. It was last call. The place was empty except for a table of woman having coffee and cake, and some men at the bar watching sports on TV. Ha-med passed by the women on his way the coat check.

"Is your grandson Evan still shtupin' that Shiksa from Jersey?" said one of the ladies.

"That wop? Gevalt no, she vas just practice." said another.

The men at the bar had had too much too drink. They spoke of the *shvartzes* with basketballs, reaching baskets and treetops.

The hostess said: "Muhammed Hassan, it was so nice to meet you, I hope you will come back and join us again."

They snickered and sneered when they heard Ha-med's name, and thought they were safe with their crude Yiddish code.

"Kuch im on!"

"Prosteh mentshent."

"A broch tsu dir!"

"Gai in drerd arein!"

Although these offensive remarks were difficult to translate, Ha-med knew what they meant.

Shit on them, those low class worthless Arabs; curse them to hell.

Ha-med just ignored them, until he heard slurs aimed at Sabira's allure.

This tall, daunting Arab handed his coat back to the hostess and stormed toward the bar. The resounding impact of his soldier-like stomps on the hard wooden floor rattled the ice in their cocktail glasses.

When Ha-med reached the bar, his sober eyes tore down their pompous esteem. He spoke Yiddish to them like a Chasidic Jew.

"*Chutzpah! Hert zich ein. Shemen zoltstu zich in dein veiten haldz. Got vaist, Got vet shtrofen! Farshtaist?*"

Proudly, he grabbed his coat and his fiancée and the striking couple strode past the admiring hostess. The silence of humiliated husbands and their embarrassed wives was deafening. They splurged for a taxi and took up one seat in the back. Sabira said: "What did you say to those men in the bar? What language was that?" He explained Yiddish to her, and translated his remarks:"What nerve! Listen here: You should be ashamed of yourselves! God knows. God will punish! Understand?"

As Sabira was drifting off to sleep in his arms, she said: "Why does God make people like that?"

"God just makes people. He lets us decide which kind we want to be."

7

Interview Day

On a muggy spring morning, Ha-med's alarm clock reminded him it was interview day. While his anxiety lay buried beneath oceans of confidence, his love for Sabira floated on clouds. The night before, he'd effortlessly carried her out of the taxi and put her to bed. He'd told her he'd be down at seven-thirty to join her for breakfast. Not quite sure if she was awake enough to remember, he set her radio for seven and left a note.

Dear Sabira-

Just some reminders:
1. Breakfast - 7:30
2. I have a train to catch - 8:50
3. Interview - 11:00
4. Wedding night - not soon enough!

Love,
Muhammed

He took a shave, trimmed his beard, showered, and as he was dressing he heard clumsy tiptoes climbing the stairs followed by a whisper.

"Ha-med, are you decent?"

He opened the door and leaned on its post. A bare-footed Sabira stood there in her sweat pants and t-shirt while balancing a tray overflowing with food. Ha-med looked, stared, and smiled. Sabira squinched her face.

"Whaaat?"

He took the tray and invited her in.

"What if your parents come up?"

"They opened Mahshi's an hour ago. Why, you're not scared of me, are you? I promise, I'll try to behave."

He gave her a kiss and set down the tray loaded with yogurt, fruit, hot rolls and fresh juice. His shirt was unbuttoned. She glanced at his chest, smiled, and shook her head with a teasing-type grin as she leaned back on the bed. He sat up on the edge and ate.

"Aren't you joining me for breakfast?" said Ha-med.

"I already ate. Besides, I could hardly carry breakfast for one."

The time was now twenty to eight. Her loose-fitting sweats and flimsy tee shirt teased Ha-med's imagination, testing his restraint. Finishing his breakfast, he lay down beside her. Their synchronized breathing intrigued Sabira but made Ha-med nervous. He thought it best that they avoid un-chaperoned intimacy.

"I'd better get ready. It's interview day." He planted a kiss on her full pouting lips, then stood up and gave her his hand.

"Walk with me to the train?"

She sat up on the edge of the bed and noticed a splash of yogurt on his chest. She smiled and grabbed a napkin. Her feet, her fingers, and her daring thoughts paused. She wanted to please him, and knew she was safe.

Open-mouthed, she encircled the spot of yogurt, then zoomed in on it with her innocent lips. She placed her hands around his waist, and then gazed up into his eyes like a sweet little puppy.

He smiled, leaned down and as he kissed her, she closed her eyes. He pulled back, admired his precious gift, and enveloped her mouth as their tongues became one. He pulled back again. This time, she leaned in and wrapped her lips around his mouth, like a student demonstrating how quickly she was getting the hang of it. Their lips locked in a union of passion. He sensed her nervousness as he helped her slip out of her shirt.

Her firm young nipples were molten with desire. Those succulent breasts and his passionate mouth formed a reverent furnace of heavenly bliss.

He eased her back down on the bed beneath him and positioned his body between her lean thighs like calm ocean waves to a sea-worthy yacht.

She had no experience with this sort of thing and grew anxious, realizing her thong became moist. As his motions soon roughened she started to panic, concerned that she wasn't quite ready. Fear sneaked up and grabbed her, then soothed her as a warmth of euphoria flushed through her veins.

The strength and the pace of his thrusting increased; she lifted her buttocks right off of the bed then she quivered and panted and started to cry. Her eyes shut, her back arched, her thighs became drenched and she trenched her hands into his muscular back. Her untarnished tingling core was ignited; her burning body first froze, then relaxed.

Sabira's fluorescent eyes cried a river of ecstatic tears as she discovered why lovers do what they do. She opened her eyes seeing his were squeezed shut and his lusting expressions made her oozing thighs boil. She imagined his hard mass was inside of her as his viscous explosion told her he was pleased.

He opened his eyes to her innocent smile. It was forever engraved in his heart and his mind. With his lips to her ear he whispered.

"Sabira, I promise to love you forever."

They relaxed a few moments. It was twenty past eight. He rinsed himself off and got dressed once again then they walked down the stairs and he kissed her goodbye.

Ha-med boarded the train, battled the crowds, rode into the city and found the address. At ten forty-five he stared up at a sign:

"McDaniel & Stoltz: *designing and building the future.*" Beneath this was an engraved bronze plaque:"The McDaniel & Stoltz Building, Owned, Operated, and Designed by McDaniel & Stoltz, dedicated to our parents."

He entered an architect's fantasy world. The office had a futuristic, art deco feel. The main lobby roof was a chrome cantilever. At his feet were massive travertine squares. To his right and his left were twin glass escalators, and between them flowed a rough granite fountain cascading around a translucent elevator. It had no cables on top and no lifts below. The mechanisms hidden behind it lent the illusion of floating upstream. Ha-med hopped on, the doors closed, and when they opened, he was in an immense open lobby with massive glass windows on three of four sides.

The reception desk rivaled a five star resort. Computers were buzzing, draftsmen were drawing and the receptionist escorted him into an office with a Persian rug, an antique desk, and a Renoir on the wall.

"Brenda, this is Mr. Muhammed Hassan. He has an eleven o'clock appointment with Mr. Stoltz." The receptionist left him with Brenda.

"Sit down, relax," said Brenda. "Mr. Stoltz is lookin' forward to meetin' you. Glowing recommendations preceded your visit. Would you like some juice, or a cold soda?"

"Thanks. No thank you. I'm fine. How about Mr. McDaniel?"

"He's the engineer ... always out and about. Checkin' sites, modifying designs. He says people make him nervous. A week could go by without even seeing his face around here. Now Stoltz, he's the architect, a real peoples person. Negotiating contracts, bidding jobs, drawing, redrawing, and drawing again. A week could go by without him ever leavin' this place. Night and day. McDaniel and Stoltz. A partnership molded in heaven. Just the opposite of my marriages, they were forged in a foundry due south of here."

Ha-med was daydreaming of "McDaniel, Stoltz, and Hassan," as Mr. Stoltz popped his head in. Ha-med rose to attention and introduced himself. Stoltz was a handsome man in his sixties wearing a blue polo shirt and light kaki trousers. Five feet nine inches tall, gray-streaked auburn hair, hazel eyes.

"It's an honor to meet you sir," said Ha-med while shaking his hand. "I appreciate you taking the time out of your busy schedule."

"My busy schedule? I was already here. I work here. I live here. You had to take the time and expense to fly here from France. You're the one to be thanked. Thank you for coming. Where are you staying?"

"I have some friends on Long Island."

"By the way, the hostess over at McDaniel's Pub called me late last night after the *incident.* You sure handled the situation. The McDaniel family and the police department go way back. So, to make a long story short, the men from the bar spent the night behind bars. DWI's. What goes around comes around?"

Mr. Stoltz and Ha-med sat down and talked.

"So, tell me about your style."

Ha-med spoke of his concept of combining steel, glass, stone slabs, and stucco. "It gives the impression that time's standing still. The future and past coalesce. As technology unfolds, you place it *next to*, not *over* what pre-existed."

Mr. Stoltz enjoyed Ha-med's concepts, confidence, and casual style.

"What is it about the world that you find most fascinating?" asked Stoltz.

"I agree with Einstein's view on that one, sir. The most incomprehensible thing about the world is that it is comprehensible."

"Bravo," said Mr. Stoltz, giving Ha-med a round of applause.

They moved to the window where an elegant telescope stood. Hand-carved mahogany, solid brass fittings, on a tripod with electronic gears.

"Come take a look at some projects."

The work locations were programmed into a computer. On the desk was a list of various projects. Mr. Stoltz punched in a number. Ha-med watched the tripod pirouette and the scope auto focus, then peered through the lens.

"That's an office complex we did in '86." The scope took another spin.

"That one's a prep school from '92." Ha-med looked and then stood back again. The scope's precision was fascinating.

"Now look closely at that iron frame construction just across from The Empire State Building." Mr. Stoltz pushed a button on his speakerphone. Ha-med squinted, focused, and saw a fearless man way up on top waltzing around on a massive steel beam. This brawny, six-foot four-inch, mustached statue-like man in a bright orange hard hat reached for his cell phone.

"Hey McDaniel, can you hear me OK?" said Stoltz.

"Crystal clear, I copy, what's up?" said McDaniel.

"I have Muhammed Hassan here with me. He's the student from the Sorbonne. Give him a wave."

Ha-med watched McDaniel waving at him then listened to their conversation. "So, What do you think? His credentials are pretty impressive, he seems to have his act together, he likes *The City*, and Brenda's first impression was good. Should we just go and offer the kid a job while he's here?" said Stoltz.

"Sure, why not? Go ahead."

Ha-med stared speechlessly at Stoltz.

"So, have some fun in New York, then go back and finish school. You have a job waiting for you when you're through."

The young architect's dream had come true. Ha-med waltzed his way through the streets of New York upon gray asphalt carpets where trucks double-parked. Yellow cabs' horns honked at red lights and stop signs and skaters and bikers and wheelchairs and trees. The elite worked from limos; the poor washed their windows, police blew their whistles and kids walked their dogs. Geometric glass giants bounced rays from the sun at the animated masses moving every which way.

On his way to the train station, Ha-med came across the Islamic Student Activities Center. Dr. Emit Dahij was already delivering his lecture when Ha-med arrived. He quietly entered and sat in the back of the sparsely populated auditorium.

" … Do good and enter the gardens. Their greeting therein is Peace," said Dahij.

A young bearded man in a black turban stood up yelling with his hands waving. "Hell is before him and he shall be given to drink from the festering water. Go back and die with your friends, the Jews!"

The professor's eyes widened, but just for a moment. He halted mid-sentence and trembled. He grasped his Koran with a quivering grip. His expression softened as security guards cuffed the heckler and hauled him away. He finished his lecture. After the talk Ha-med greeted Dahij. They chatted a bit, and then with a handshake, Ha-med thanked him, and went on his way.

Just one more year and Ha-med would be out of school with a Master's degree, a superb job and a stunning young wife. His future seemed perfect.

8

Dilemma

Ha-med eagerly shared his employment news with the Ibrahims, whose overflowing exuberance bounced from laughter to tears and then back to laughter again.

When Sabira and Ha-med took a break from uncontrollable giggling and hugging, he ran to the phone and called Haifa. The phone just kept ringing. He just kept holding. When Shaina finally picked up the phone, Ha-med realized that in Israel, the time was 4 a.m.

"Shalom?" said Shaina in a slow groggy voice.

"Hey Shaina, it's Ha-med. Sorry, I forgot that it's late, or early or – "

"Ha-med? Is that you? Is everything alright?" she nudged Yoav. "It's Ha-med, wake up."

"Guess what? I have a job waiting for me in New York City at McDaniel and Stoltz as soon as I graduate."

"Mazel Tov! You deserve it." While still half asleep, Yoav pulled at the phone.

"Is he OK? Is everything alright with Ha-med?" Shaina told Yoav the news and he yanked the phone out of her hands.

"Mazel Tov, Mazel Tov. We are so proud of you!"

Shaina and Yoav continued their phone-cord tug-of-war.

"Oh, and Sabira is a dream come true. I'm not quite sure what I've done to deserve such a gift. You will fall in love with her the moment you meet her, which I hope is soon."

"Hey, Ha-med, if you get a chance, would you go by and visit my mother?" said Shaina.

"I will. I'll call you from Paris in a couple of days, bye-bye."

Sabira's eyes moistened when she heard him say, "Paris in a couple of days."

The Ibrahims' happy round faces lengthened and saddened as well. He sat close to Sabira, grasped both her hands, looked intensely at her parents, and spoke.

"The love Sabira and I share is no secret; it is endless, and our parting will be a great burden. To seek your permission for Sabira to spend the summer in France is something I desire, but would not dare request. Our temptation is strong and our bodies are weak. To wait almost two more years is an agony I could not endure."

The tick of the wall clock, the refrigerator's hum and the drip of the sink filled the small silent room. Ha-med stood up, faced Sabira's parents and continued.

"I ask for Sabira's hand after the summer, as she turns seventeen."

Sabira jumped up into his arms and covered him with kisses. Mrs. Ibrahim tried hiding her smile of approval. Mr. Ibrahim was not sure how to respond, and wished not to act impulsively. He said he would need a day to think it over. He stood up, shook his head, and walked into his room to the echoes of giggles and kisses.

"Shhhhh, my children. Behave. You are not yet married!" said Mrs. Ibrahim as she smiled, shrugged her shoulders, winked, and followed her husband.

A moment later Ha-med tapped on their door, gave them each a hug and asked to borrow the car to go to the mosque. Momar looked at the clock.

"It's getting late. The final Jumma Prayer is about to begin. Drive safely … but hurry!" he said.

Dead silence echoed from inside the mosque. All were bowed down, prepared to begin the Ishaa. Ha-med raced up to the heavy double wooden doors and gave them a shove. They flew open with a resounding crash. Everyone inside sprang to his feet in a stance of defense, prepared to respond to a threat.

When the Imam saw that it was Ha-med, he looked at his watch.

"We have been waiting for you. I guess now we can begin our prayers."

When the service ended, the Imam invited Ha-med to join him

up front and presented him to the congregation. After brief introductions, Ha-med shared his thoughts with the room.

His articulate tongue captured the crowd in a refreshing hypnotic trance. He spoke of Sabira, his school, architecture, Bassan, his childhood, Israel, France, and quoted the Koran, Frank Lloyd Wright, and Mark Twain.

He was informative, entertaining, and tossed in a pinch of humor.

"When I first moved to Paris, waiters looked at me funny. I requested my desserts in the Allah mode. I thought Pie 'a la mode' was an Islamic Pastry".

He held the congregation's rapt attention. The elders were likewise enthralled.

When the crowd had dispersed, the only people left were Ha-med, the Imam and a man named Afridi. This wise, learned man was the oldest member of the congregation and those privileged to know him were blessed.

Five-feet-four-inches and a hundred and sixty pounds of pious unselfish wisdom. He had a wife for seven decades, together since youth. When she passed away he mourned for three days and nights, praised Allah and never shed another tear.

He celebrated her life in lieu of mourning her death. Afridi outlived both of his children and responded in the same fashion when they passed on. He referred to it as, "rolling with the punches that God throws our way."

Ha-med and Afridi shared an immediate fondness. He reminded Ha-med so much of Bassan. "Ha-med, I am old, they call me old-fashioned," said Afridi in a grandfatherly tone. "You know who you remind me of? Me. You remind me of me many decades ago. You would be a great asset here. An example, an inspiration, a role model for our youth. "We have difficulty getting young men to attend the mosque," said the Imam. "They want to blend in with their friends. No time for Koran. No! No interest in Islam. They'd rather dance, play ball, and be just like the others. They permit non-believers to pollute their brains."

"I'm so sorry, but I'm leaving for Paris on Sunday," said Ha-med, not sure if he was relieved or disappointed. "I must go and finish school."

As the Imam and Afridi walked Ha-med out to his car, the Imam said, "Why of course you must go, but good news travels fast. We have been told that you have a great job lined up in the city when you graduate."

"Oh, by the way, Ha-med," said Afridi, while patting Ha-med on the back. "The Imam and I offer congratulations to you and your *young* bride," Ha-med scratched his head as Afridi continued. "Mr. Ibrahim was hesitant to allow his daughter to marry before her eighteenth year, so he called us this evening to request our guidance. So, what do you think? What should we advise the concerned father who trusts our opinion? See you at the mosque when you return?"

The next morning Ha-med and Sabira were granted permission to marry whenever their hearts so desired.

Mr. Ibrahim explained to them, "Yesterday evening when you left, I was troubled, so I sought the advice of a wise old friend. We spoke a little while before Ishaa. Late last night, he called me and spoke of the inspiration he'd received during prayer. He explained to me that we know not when our short visit on earth nears its finale. It is not man's place to delay tranquility between those who Allah has chosen to let love."

Sabira hugged her parents and then embraced her husband-to-be.

"Just remember what your mother told you last night. You are not yet married!" Mr. Ibrahim said.

Ha-med asked Sabira whether she would object to visiting Shaina's mother. Sabira suddenly emitted a newfound glow of maturity.

"Whatever shall please you, my Ha-med."

He took a phone number from his wallet and called Mrs. Leibowitz. She answered "Hello," in a strong Yiddish accent.

"Good afternoon, Mrs. Leibowitz. My name is Muhammed Hassan, and I am a friend of your daughter Shaina."

She cut him off mid-sentence.

"Cha-med? Is that you? My Shainala has told me so much about you. So? Where are you? Are you here? Are you coming to visit?"

"Yes, Mrs. Leibowitz. I am here on Long Island. May I come by and visit with my fiancée, Sabira? Will you be at home for a while?"

"Vy sure, and vy not? I will kensel my hot date. So, you know where to find the Long Island Expressway?" She proceeded to provide lengthy detailed directions.

As he drove through Bayside in the Borough of Queens he was overwhelmed by the diversity of signage and culture. Kosher, Hallel, Spanish, Chinese, Haitian, mosques, temples, synagogues, shrines. They followed the directions to Bay Terrace and drove through an area crowded with apartments, a sprawling shopping center, two country clubs, and a school. They found the building, and parked a few blocks away. As they entered the lobby, an overwhelmingly pleasant five-foot-two-inch, blue-haired dynamo greeted them.

"And you must be Muhammed, and this *maidle-a* is your Sabira? And such a jewel. So? Tell me? How were my directions? Did you have any trouble finding it?"

The three boarded a small elevator and by the time they got off on the sixteenth floor they were like family. At the end of the hallway was a metal door with three locks, a peephole, and a mezuzah.

Mrs. Liebowitz touched the mezuzah, kissed her fingers, unlocked the door, and welcomed them in. The small apartment had a delightful breezy terrace. A Steinway upright, covered with family photos, stood in one corner.

They sat down at the dining room table and Mrs. Leibowitz spoke incessantly for twenty minutes about her Shaina and her husband Morris who had died of a heart attack ten years before. She spoke of her son, the principal at a high school in Brooklyn; of his wife, and of her three talented grandchildren.

"So? I've been doing all the talking. Tell me, what about your plans? Shaina says you're going to be an architect? And what a *mensch* you are. You are studying in Paris? My Morris, may he rest in peace, and I once went to Paris, but that was years ago. And Yoav? How is he? Are you hungry? Would you like I should take out a cake?

When Mrs. Leibowitz finally tired out, Ha-med and Sabira spoke of their plans.

"Shaina fondly recalls drifting off to sleep to the soothing sounds of your piano," Ha-med said. "She said you were a very talented musician and a popular teacher as well."

Mrs. Leibowitz smiled as she remembered too, though the memory seemed distant and blurred.

"Do you still play?" said Sabira.

"When I was about the same age as you are, my piano and I were best friends. I would fall asleep still playing," said Mrs. Leibowitz.

"Play something for me?" said Sabira.

Mrs. Leibowitz walked up to her Steinway and played a Mozart Sonata while Sabira waded through a stack of old dusty songbooks.

She came across a collection of duets and found a composition that she and her teacher had performed in a jazz competition, a ragtime medley of Scott Joplin Music arranged for four hands.

She thumbed through the music to refresh her memory as Mrs. Leibowitz curtsied, smiled and began to walk away from the piano.

"And maestro, where do you think you are going?" asked Sabira as she set the duet on the piano. "Would you play this for me?"

Mrs. Leibowitz, unaware that Sabira played, said: "*Tzatskehleh*, that's a duet, for four hands."

"Yes, I know. So? Which part do you want?"

Mrs. Leibowitz took bass and Sabira sat up on top.

"Mamala, let's see what you've got!" Sabira laughed.

Ha-med sat back as the women played on, laughing and impressing one another to no end. When they finished, they hugged and Ha-med gave them a standing ovation.

"It's time for some lunch," said Ha-med. "Would you two lovely ladies care to join me?"

"Only on one condition. It's my treat," said Mrs. Leibowitz.

They walked over to a deli where waiters with bow ties, white shirts and black vests raced through the crowd delivering coleslaw, pickles, Dr. Brown's sodas and towering sandwiches.

"I just can't decide – brisket or chicken?" said Sabira

Mrs. Leibowitz was delighted to provide her advice.

"First have a cup of chicken soup, then a nice piece of brisket. Two birds mit one stone? No, actually, one bird, and a cow!"

One table over sat a mother, father and their two cute pubescent boys who struggled not to seem obvious as they admired Sabira.

Mrs. Leibowitz leaned over and whispered so only they could hear: "You want I should run out and buy you a camera?"

"So boys, what will it be?" said their father. After they ordered, their father said to one of them: "So, are you ready for your Bar-Mitzvah next month?" Remember, our trip to Israel this summer is a reward for the effort and work you've been putting in."

As Mrs. Leibowitz's fine-tuned undercover skills honed in on their conversation, she couldn't resist joining in.

She turned her chair in their direction

"My daughter and her husband live in Haifa. He's a lawya. Studied here at Columbia."

The young mother, a very attractive woman in her early thirties, turned and said, "We will be spending two days in Haifa. I hear it is beautiful."

"Heaven on Earth," said Ha-med as he handed her a business card from Bassan's.

"If you get a chance, stop by. It's my shop. Ask for Shaina Goldstein."

As they got up to leave, Dr. and Mrs. Benjamin Meyer and their boys thanked them for their warmth. Ha-med wished them a magnificent visit to Israel, which they had, followed by several jubilant years.

As each year passed, the happy couple's relationship would mellow like a fine vintage wine, but on one dreadful morning the cork would dislodge when Dr. Meyer would go for that fatal last run.

9

Mourning

A week had inched by since that sad, awful day when a doctor had gone jogging; a woman had given birth. A widow named Carole and her two teenage sons would have to somehow adjust to a fatherless home. A man named Muhammed would have much to explain to his newborn Aneesa whose mother was gone.

A blinding orange sunset accompanied wailing Arabic prayers as Sabira's grieving parents sat engulfed in disbelief.

White-knuckled, Ha-med's fists rested firmly on the tabletop, his head wedged between them. Anguish ripped a crevice deep within his broken heart.

Ever resilient, they would turn to Aneesa to subdue their internal Jihad.

In the tradition of their ancestors, Grandpa took a pasty fresh date from his mouth and placed it on her palate. Then Grandma cut off her wispy black hair. They laid Aneesa down on her belly and she struggled to lift her head.

Refusing to concede, she struggled and failed again and again. A glimmer of a grin snuck through her father's solemn eyes as he sunk into the couch and rested his head back on Mrs. Ibrahim's shoulder. In a moment of twilight, neither awake nor asleep, childhood visions formed fresh in his mind.

The Hassans lived in an impoverished village on the border between Israel and Jordan. They were better off than most of their neighbors, blessed with health, shelter, family and food. From a lineage of stonemasons legends were told of the palatial fortresses Ha-med's ancestors built.

While mothers did house chores from dusk until dawn, fathers went off and worked weeks at a time. His father found steady work in both Israel and Jordan. His mother struggled to provide a home for her two children and her mother-in-law.

Ha-med and his sister Aneesa were best friends. Smack in the midst of their sandbox-like village was the children's playground. It consisted of wooden munitions crates, two railroad ties, an oversized tire and an overturned jeep.

On a breezy spring afternoon, Grandma sat watching the children at play. A dozen were running and laughing, then suddenly froze. They observed a car the likes of which they had never seen before. It was longer than the few they had seen, like two vehicles merged into one.

A motionless driver was glued to the wheel and a pair of armed, statue-silent soldiers sat braced in the back.

When the car stopped, its roof mysteriously opened and an ominous giant rose. His flowing beard coalesced with his turban and robe.

To Muhammad, the man seemed weathered, ancient, evil and scary although he couldn't have been much older than 30.

The villagers gathered as the ground trembled to the sheik's booming oratory:

"*Assalam alaikum,*" said Sheik Ahmed Muhammed Khalil. "Allah has commanded me to be his messenger. For the souls of our sainted martyrs, we shall exterminate the Zionist presence and drive the Jews into the sea. The armies of Iraq, Algeria, Kuwait, Sudan, and the whole Arab Nation stand with us. It is Jihad Time!"

As the Sheik grinned psychotically at Muhammed, a shiver crawled up the boy's spine. It was then that Muhammed noticed the Sheik's crippled left hand. It had only three fingers and these were scarred, twisted and bent with no fingertips. His thumb was flattened, with no fingernail.

Ha-med and Aneesa ran into their grandmother's arms. "Why do we want Israel to die? Isn't that where father finds his best work?" said Muhammed.

"Don't they have little kids like my brother and me?" said his sister. Grandmother squeezed them tightly as she wept.

Muhammed's slumber that night was filled with horrific images and the sheik was reduced to a vivid nightmare. His young mind decided he didn't exist. Young Ha-med awoke in a sweat – the blurred image of a car, a mysterious figure and a monstrous hand were stored away with vague memories of dragons and ghosts.

A few days later, a caravan of soldiers no older than 17 ripped through the small village. Thunderous shrieks of "Jihad!" echoed as they rode toward Israel, shooting bullets into the sky.

A week passed. Explosions and gunfire followed dreary truckloads of drawn out faces back through the village.

Shattered souls and bashed heads drowned in dense clouds of sand. There were no more cheers of "Jihad," no more shots fired in the air. Once mighty spirits now fragile and broken along with their hearts and their bones.

Some were dead, some were dying; some were Jews, some were Arabs. To Muhammed, they all looked the same. Ha-med's bare feet ached from the ground's endless muted rumbling.

"Mother? Father? Aneesa? Grandmother?"

The cold sound of death echoed back. People were being stopped, being searched, some arrested, some shot. Loud shrieking screams filled the air.

Tormented by his fragility, and sickened by the stench of dismembered remains, Ha-med wandered until his body gave out.

He awoke to more rumbling, sweating profusely. Some soldiers tossed him a canteen and some bread. No one to stop him, no one to love him. He made it to the old Arab quarter in Jerusalem and collapsed in the arms of Bassan.

Stinging beads of perspiration dripped from his forehead into his eyes. He was dazed, confused, lost. He wiped his eyes and found himself on the living room couch with his head propped up on a pillow, his mother-in-law sobbing, and his daughter asleep in Mr. Ibrahim's arms.

At the Meyer's home, the week crawled by like a heart wrenching lamenting monotonous fugue.

On the eighth morning, David greeted the sunrise, ground some coffee beans and joined Andrew by the stove, emotions barely percolating.

Their mother awoke and the affect-less trio sat in a row, staring out at the yard. A dormant grass field lay at the feet of bare trees where last season's soggy foliage decayed. The sky's pastel-gray hue reflected on the pool with dead leaves of winter dotting its surface. A solid oak swing hung from an old tree. Beneath it the grass no longer grows from generations of scraping heels.

Andrew was the first to stand up from the table. He surveyed the home, assessed the damage and spoke.

"Plates, silverware, chairs and tables, usually stacked in the closet. Sheets on mirrors, usually on beds. Lots of food stacked everywhere. So, where do we begin?"

"I guess we can uncover the mirrors … try not to scream!" said Mother.

In Jewish tradition, mirrors are covered during the week of mourning, called "*sitting shivah*." As they disrobed the mirrors, it was hard for them not to grin at their disheveled appearance.

Everywhere they looked, food was piled on platters. David was the last to interrupt his silence.

"We have enough surplus food here to feed several small nations."

Brief smiles appeared, then faded. Andrew observed the food to be wasted. He spoke to his mother in his grandfather's accent.

"*Vat*, are you crazy? Your eyes are bigger than your stomach."

David picked up where his brother left off.

"*Vat a shandeh un a charpeh*."

Which was Grandfather's way of saying *a shame and a disgrace.*

Mother came in right on cue.

"You vaste all this food? There are children in Europe mit noting to eat?"

The three found the courage. They smiled and hugged and then laughed out loud. A silent storm came crashing down. This trio remembered they had been a quartet. Their grins turned to frowns and they huddled and wept.

The boy's hearts were torn, but they grieved for their mother's loss more than for their own.

David accompanied his sobbing mother to her room. Andrew sat down on the fireplace hearth and stared at photographs from his youth on the mantle. Above the mantelpiece was a family portrait from a time and a place now distant and vague. The crackling embers sent fireflies dancing. He reclined on the couch and drifted to sleep with the flickering cinders fresh in his mind.

He found himself at their family campsite in front of a lake, singing and playing guitar with a campfire glowing, stars in the sky. The fireflies he had trapped in a jar were on top of a pole like a lantern.

"Guess I'll call it a night," his mother said.

"Me too," said David. "We've got a full day of hiking and canoeing tomorrow."

Father and Andrew relaxed by the fire.

"So Andrew, two more years till your Bar Mitzvah. And then what?" Any ideas for your future?"

"Well, I really love music – singin', playin', listening. Maybe I'll be a famous rock star?"

"Music's fine. I love it too," said Dr. Meyer, as he reached for the guitar and strummed a few chords. "But Andrew, it's not all that glamour you see on MTV. Millions try, a handful strike it rich. So … if music is your choice, be the best, work hard – and go to college! That way, at least while you're striving for fame and fortune, you can teach; be a professor; make a living."

"Do you think Mom will get mad when I tell her I don't want to be a doctor?"

"We can't all be doctors, there'd be too many of us. Wouldn't be enough sick people to go around."

Ya wanna talk proud Jewish mothers? Neil Diamond's, Carol King's, Barry Manilow's, Carly Simon's, Simon's and Garfunkel's. Bob Dylan's. Now we're talkin' proud. And your mother and I saw them all. Boy, did we go to concerts!"

"How'd you guys meet, anyway?"

"Well Andrew, my grandfather was a fine tailor. The finest. An artist with needle and thread. And your mother's grandfather liked fine clothing. The finest. His wardrobe *was* fine art.

"So when Grandpa Charlie needed something special, he'd stop by the shop. When my father was learning his craft, long before he opened his own clothing store, I would join him at work, sit up on the stool, and watch my grandpa – your great grandfather – teach him the tricks of the trade.

"One day I was kinda' watchin', kinda' bored, and I saw a car pull up. A shinny Pierce Arrow.

Grandpa quickly organized his wares, fixed dad's collar, brushed off his coat, straightened out a little, and continued to work, as if he hadn't noticed the car. The uniformed driver walked around and opened the passenger door. Out strolled the man who would one day become my Grandpa Charlie.

"Alongside him was his granddaughter, an angel. The most beautiful thing I had ever seen, even with crooked teeth. I can still remember her smile, even back then.

"Although years would pass before we'd be formally introduced, I swear I knew that very day, the very first time I laid eyes on her. I was going to marry her. I wasn't even supposed to like girls yet. I was thirteen. She was eleven."

While Dr. Meyer was reminiscing and dreaming out loud, Andrew closed his eyes, but not his ears. Benjamin laid him back, looked up at the stars, and continued to speak

"The Cohens and Meyers were from different backgrounds, different countries, and their people had been victimized by different cultures, but for the same reason: they were Jews.

"Carole's Grandpa Charlie was Orthodox, kosher, born in a Russian Shtetyl … that's a self-sustaining little village. A butcher, baker, rabbi, y'know? Like 'Fiddler on the Roof'"?

"The villagers were told, three days in advance to pack up and leave. They were tired of being warned, tired of being uprooted, tired of being threatened, tired of running. They were just plain tired. They loaded their wagons and saddlebags to the brim. Not with clothing and goods, but with sticks, bricks, rakes and shovels. On a calm, snowy Sabbath a parade of Russians on horseback arrived to escort the Jews out of their homes. In a clever attempt to ambush the invaders, they reached for their weapons. They even struck down a few.

"Then sword-bearing Cossacks with Molotov Cocktails descended upon them like sharks to fresh blood. The women and children took shelter and witnessed the blood spewing out beneath clamoring hooves.

"The Rabbi was torched along with his temple. With assistance from the Hebrew Immigrant Aid Society (HIAS) Grandpa Cohen managed to negotiate his way to America, and move in with an uncle."

Benjamin Meyer's grandfather was a reform Jew, born in Germany, and proud of his German heritage. His family had lived there for 500 years.

A skilled tailor, and a shrewd businessman, he catered to the upper class, and lived well in the middle class. He owned a two-story building on an upscale Berlin street.

His home was upstairs and his business was downstairs. As he approached fifty, his life was content. Two daughters, a son, and a beautiful wife.

But a cloud without a silver lining hovered over his pleasant existence, and one day a tempest blew right through his walls. The tempest was Hitler. His reign drowned Mankind in a deluge of hate.

The building was invaded by S.S. officers. His young son was tossed out a window for sport. The boy's skull hit the ground, splitting like a Halloween pumpkin; his blood filled the cracks of the cobblestone street.

His wife was shot dead while his daughters were raped and his building was claimed by the "Aryan Race."

It churned out outfits for soldiers and suits for commanders, swastikas for Nazis and stars the Jews. Each morning he woke to the sickening stench of smoldering flesh upon piles of death.

Upon camp liberation his emaciated body was greeted by Liberty's torch-bearing light. Shortly after arrival in New York, he met a woman. She was twenty years younger, but looked twice her age. Her story from Auschwitz was a heart-wrenching tale of using her body to keep her alive. They consoled one another and Samuel was born. Grandpa Meyer passed on, and Samuel opened a clothing store. "Samuel's" always did *all right.* Never great. Never bad. Always just *all right.*

From time to time Carole's Father would frequent the shop, and speak of his daughter and Mr. Samuel Meyer would speak of his son Benjamin.

Carole's father, Dr. Cohen was not as religious as was her grandfather Charlie, not so orthodox; followed more conservative Jewish customs. Samuel Meyer, on the other hand became more observant than his father had been. Followed more conservative Jewish customs.

One Yom Kippur, the Cohens and Meyers went to the same temple. They had fasted, and were famished. When sundown fell, the adults leisurely strolled to the banquet hall to break their fast. The teenage boys acted as if the bell at Aqueduct Race Track had rung and the rabbit was in the lead. Like a stampede they leaped hurdles and trotted to the food.

Sixteen year-old Benjamin Meyer was a gifted runner, a track star, and as guilty as the rest. He flew from the chapel ahead of the heat, down the steps two at a time, and with a hand on the railing, made a sharp turn. He skidded, and stopped dead in his tracts. Standing across the room with three other giggling thirteen year-old girls was Carole Cohen. Her smile hadn't changed. Her braces sparkled. Her precocious figure made young teenage boys blush. As he stood staring, Carole's parents approached her, and Benjamin's approached him.

"Benjamin, we are so very proud of you. While your friends ran to devour the food like *vilder chei-eh* (wild animals), you stood here and patiently waited for us. What a *mentsh*." Just then, Dr. and Mrs. Cohen took their daughter Carole by the hand and walked her over to greet the Meyer family.

"*Gut Yontev*. Happy New Year," said Dr. Cohen.

"And a *Gut Yontev* to you, and to yours, *Lishonoh tovah*. You've already met my wife. This is our son, Benjamin. He says he wants to be a doctor, a surgeon."

"It is a pleasure to meet you, Benjamin. I knew your grandfather. What a *choshever mentsh (fine lovable man)*, and the finest tailor I ever knew. I guess you've got stitching in you genes. Here is my card, call me some time. I'll show you around the hospital. Peak in on some surgery?"

"Thank you sir. I would like that."

"This is my wife, Mrs. Cohen. And this is our daughter, Carole.

Vants to be an ectress she says."

Carole and Benjamin stared at each other like Merlin had caste upon them a lover's spell. They strolled to the punchbowl ahead of their parents. He poured two glasses, gathered some bagels with all the fixings, and they sat down.

"D'ya know, we met once a couple of years ago. Your grandfather brought you to my grandfathers tailor shop. You drove up in a fancy car, with your own driver? I think you were about ten?"

"I was eleven!"

"So ... you do remember?" Wanna know what I told Gramps when you left?"

"Le'me guess. Whose that funny lookin' kid who needs braces?"

"Nope. I told him I was going to marry you."

"So, what did your Grandpa say?"

"Do you understand Yiddish?"

"That's what he said?"

"No. Do you?"

"Do I what?"

"Understand Yiddish?"

When Benjamin realized this pretty, witty, younger woman was teasing him, they smiled at each other and started to laugh. He looked at her smile and she looked into his eyes. They're brains did not know how to deal with their hearts.

"Fun dein moyl in Gots oyern! That's what grandpa said. It means from your lips to God's ears."

"I know what it means. It's Yiddish."

Benjamin noticed her juice cup was empty. He stood up.

"Can I get you some more punch?"

"Yes, please. I'll join you."

They felt together, alone in a fog of enchantment. As he reached for her glass, their hands brushed. He never knew hands could be so warm. Neither did she. His shook a little. So did hers. They both experienced their first crush. For Benjamin, it was the only crush he ever had.

After that day, they occasionally crossed paths, mostly during High Holy days at Shul, but they lived in different neighborhoods, different worlds. He went to public schools; She went to private. His father sold fine clothing. Her father bought fine clothing. His vacations were to the Catskills and Miami. Hers were to The Alps and Maui.

Several years later at a Temple Purim Party they chatted, danced, and became inseparable. She was a junior, skipped a year, planning to attend Wellesley. He was a senior, getting ready to start City College, Pre-med, on a track and field scholarship. She had come with some other girls, driven by their parents. He was already driving; had his own car; a five year-old red Camero convertible; a high school graduation gift from his parents. When the party ended, they walked outside together, holding hands, sharing hearts, to shy to kiss.

"Can I give you a ride home?"

"No? My parents would just die. Sheryl's mom is on her way. If I'm not in that car, I might as well not go home."

"Would you be my date for the senior prom?"

"Yes? I mean yes!"

Carole saw Sheryl's mom pulling up, and gave Benjamin a quick peck on his cheek before she fluttered away. Summer brought with it a summer romance. His days were spent as a tailor with dad. Hers were spent waiting for him to get home. Summertime ended and he started City College. A year later, she started Wellesley. A week after that, they spent the weekend in Boston. When he left, they were engaged.

Against her parent's wishes, warnings, hopes and prayers, they got married on her eighteenth birthday. She lived in Massachusetts. He was in New York. Their long distance romance and once a month love was magical, wonderful, brazen, and fun. They were like kids. They were kids. Soul-mates from the day he first saw her crooked little teeth. In three years she earned an economics degree and he entered NYU Medical School. They lived in The Village and both studied hard. He learned anatomy. She learned Lamaze. He got straight A's. She had two boys.

For exercise, relaxation, transportation, and fun, he ran. It was his passion. Short distance, long distance, marathons, winter, summer. Didn't matter. Aside from his wife and the boys, it was what he loved most. He died doing what he loved.

10

Time

Time is a stubborn, insensitive thing.
Implore it to hasten?
It crawls.
Beseech it to dawdle? It soars.
At epochs of sorrow, it slams on its brakes.

Five years passed by since Benjamin went for his final jog. Before that, Carole Meyer was *living.* Now she *existed* in her echoing home accompanied by memories and ghosts. The children went off to college. Her philanthropic efforts continued, though their flames became dim. On a magnificent Sunday she awoke feeling tense. Her sons both phoned her (as they always did on Sunday mornings), and she said she was fine.

She strolled through her home and although it was perfect, she organized, arranged things, and cleaned out the fridge. With no plans for the day, she went for a drive and her car found its' way to the Charles Cohen Clinic. She parked and paced into the meditation garden. She was greeted by the flowers and their sweet morning scent. The fog was thinning, letting the sun light the dew-coated leaves. Carole stared through the fog at the brick by her feet that her grandfather dedicated to her almost forty-two years before. She read it aloud: "A Baby is God's Opinion That The World Should Go On."

She thought she was alone. The sound of a tender young voice startled her. "Daddy, Who's that pretty lady?" said Aneesa.

Carole gazed up at the sweetest face that she had ever seen. Aneesa stepped back; her pudgy lips smiled. In her rose-colored dress and satin bow she looked like a Fifth Avenue window display. She backed up to the bench and hopped onto her father's knee. He said: "We do not know her. Why don't you go and ask her?"Aneesa jumped down and walked up to Carole.

"Hello, pretty lady, my name is Aneesa. My father said I could come ask you your name. Ha-med tried hard not to stare. Carole and Aneesa shook hands. "Pleased to meet you young lady. My name is Carole."

Aneesa continued to make conversation as Ha-med looked on both amused and engrossed. "I was born at this hospital five years ago," said Aneesa.

"Well then, young lady, we sure do have something in common. I was born here too," said Carole.

Aneesa's smile, exaggerated expressions and angelic voice made Carole melt. She glanced towards Ha-med. He was admiring her. He could not ignore her tight tailored jeans and the body they clung too. She was flattered. She smiled. He smiled back. Their eyes locked. He blinked and looked down. Aneesa jumped back on his knee.

"You and your daughter sure look cute together. I always had wished for a daughter."

"Do you have any children?"

"Two sons, both off in college."

Aneesa listened, giggled and hopped off his knee as Ha-med stood up and faced Carole, who couldn't help notice his cute naïve shyness. It was as if he didn't realize how handsome he was. The sun's reflection on Carole golden-brown hair haloed her face and lit up her eyes. Her thick glossy lips made Ha-med's lips feel dry so he licked them not intending to appear flirtatious. Their eyes met again and exchanged glows of warmth. Aneesa tugged on daddy's sleeve and he leaned down towards her. She whispered into his ear while grabbing his sleeve.

"Daddy, why don't you tell her your name?"

He shook Carole's warm hand. "I am Muhammed Hassan. They call me Ha-med and you've already met my shy little daughter."

"Pleased to meet you Ha-med ... Have we ever met?"

"I too get the feeling we have crossed paths."

With a pleasant awkward pensive expression, she smiled, and then glanced down at her watch.

"I've got to be going. My name is Meyer, Carole Meyer. I come here quite often." She smiled, turned and walked off. His eyes were glued to her every move. She spun her head towards him, her flowing hair followed. She caught him again. She gave him a smile and then turned and strolled off.

11

McDaniel & Stoltz

The loud crack of dawn startled Ha-med while Aneesa ignored it and slept right on through. He went to the bathroom and stared at the mirror. Its' fog obscured his view. He used his palm to unveil his reflection, which softened again in a haze of fresh mist. The mirror reflected glimmers of hope as the impressionist image whispered to him: "Sabira is gone, your life must go on."

His wife had been gone for half a decade and his five-year old daughter taught him to take one day at a time. He dressed her up, packed her lunch, and drove her to school. She held Daddy's hand as he walked her to class. With a hug and a kiss he said: "I love you, little angel. Wait right her for Grandma after school."

"Daddy, how come you say that every day?"

He drove off to work. It was his refuge. An architect's Disneyland. They built everything from skyscrapers to homes. A decade had passed since he first joined the firm and he prayed to be partner before the year's end.

The present day owners, McDaniel and Stoltz owe it all to their parents who started with ziltch. McDaniel's father served bar in a small Irish pub. When its owner passed on, the old building foreclosed. He borrowed some money and kept the place going and he and his wife struggled to make ends meet. Prohibition nearly wiped them out. They survived serving sodas, and burgers, and floats and ignoring patrons' hip flasks poured into their cokes.

At the same time, his friend Stoltz owned a small butcher shop. The inspectors and unions made it hard to survive. One year at Thanksgiving the Stoltzs and McDaniels sat down after lunch. Stoltz had a brainstorm.

"Let's each save some money, and invest in some land."

"Cheers, I'll drink to that!" said McDaniel. Their grandiose strategy was blurred by the eggnog; by sunrise their hangovers foiled the plan.

Days, months and years hurried by since that Thanksgiving dinner. Each worked hard and prospered as their businesses grew. The small butcher shop had become "Stoltz Fine Purveyors of Provisions and Meats." The wholesale division purchased freezer trucks and began distribution along the east coast.

The small neighborhood pub had the luck of the Irish. In the right place at the right time when prohibition ended. Theatre folks flocked there and critics would mingle. McDaniel's served Stoltz's fine steaks by the ton. The walls became plastered with celebrity photos bearing personal thanks for their wonderful meals. Busloads of tourists would squeeze their way in hoping to catch a quick glimpse of a star. Nighttime's live jazz attracted two sorts. Lovers would cuddle and dance to soft music while lonely ones drank, all alone at the bar.

McDaniel and Stoltz were both frugal and smart. At another Thanksgiving they passed on the eggnog and worked out the details of "McDaniel and Stoltz." They invested in small bits of land in New York. During the depression they had money to spare. They bought up as much of New York as they could. As the hard times gave way to more prosperous years they leased and sold land, and their fortune was born.

As coincidence would have it, they each had a son. Ethan McDaniel and Steven M. Stoltz were bonded like brothers, but they bypassed the sibling rivalry stage. Their personalities merged like two halves of a whole. Steven was outgoing, popular with the ladies, a real peoples person. Ethan was quiet. He kept to himself. Didn't date much.

Young Steven Stoltz designed buildings with blocks. His Lincoln Log castles were true works of art. As a teen he sketched dream homes that some day he would build; he placed Frank Lloyd Wright just a smidge below God. While completing his undergraduate studies at Stanford, he met a potter named Amy, whose major was art. Raised in

Los Angeles to working class parents, she and her 4 siblings all graduated from college.

Steven and Amy followed their dream to Rhode Island School of Design. They received their Masters degrees. His was in architecture, hers was in teaching. They both loved big city lights, action, and excitement. They married and then purchased a brownstone in the heart of The Big Apple with plenty of room – for the three sons and two daughters that they someday would have.

As a child, Ethan McDaniel's erector set cities were like no others. As a teen, his favorite spectator-sport was construction. While others cheered baseball, this tall quiet loaner would applaud those in hardhats suspended from heaven on massive steel beams. Ethan went off to M.I.T. to pursue a mechanical engineering degree.

One Sunday afternoon Ethan wandered around Boston Common, negotiating his way through street musicians, pushcart vendors, and evangelical fanatics. He realized he was being followed – by a frisky young pedigree collie. Ethan kneeled down and the puppy approached. The two took an immediate liking to each other. A few moments later a concerned voice echoed through the crowds.

"Sylvia, bad dog. Where have you been? Good thing for you there are no more gallows around here!"

The puppy whimpered, Ethan laughed, and then out of nowhere, it started to pour. The three ducked for cover beneath a coffee shop awning.

"I hope Sylvia wasn't a bother", said Susan.

"Bother? She was so worried. She was looking all over for you," said Ethan.

That happenstance meeting on a soggy Sunday formed the glue for an inseparable union. Susan, a veterinary student at Tufts, was raised by strict parents on a farm in Kentucky. She was an only child. Home schooled. Sheltered. Her parents bred horses and collies. Ethan and Susan finished school, were married on her family's ranch, and then purchased an equestrian estate in Sands Point, Long Island. Their limitless love was reserved for their horses, collies, and each other. It left no room to raise children.

Steven Stoltz and Ethan McDaniel proudly followed in their father's footsteps. From a butcher shop, a pub, and humble roots arose the second generation of, "McDaniel and Stoltz". Their first project was an office tower built on family land, using money that their parents were glad to invest. It housed their headquarters on the top floor and beneath it were offices, shops, and places to dine.

Years later, they made the decision of a lifetime: they hired Muhammed Hassan.

Ha-med hopped off the elevator with a cheerful good morning. He found a new project was waiting for him. *Renovation of building, project M1263.* A meeting with McDaniel and Stoltz was scheduled weeks in advance. He grabbed up his laptop, cell phone, palm pilot and headed over to the conference room. The sliding glass doors automatically closed, the windows magically darkened and a flat screen high definition television descended from the ceiling. Ha-med took a seat in his usual place, followed by Brenda and Stoltz.

"McDaniel couldn't make it, so I guess we'll get started," said Mr. Stoltz. "This hospital building was a glowing example of philanthropy in its day. The structure itself was called "modern" back then. The architect's concept was *simple yet grand.* Avoid impersonal sharp angles by incorporating relaxing curves, arches, rounded edges, and a rotunda for the lobby. An educational wing was added a few years ago."

The screen above their heads lit up and displayed the project they were competing for. It was an extensive renovation. As the building appeared on the screen, Ha-med's stared in disbelief. His eyebrows reached the ceiling and his jaw slammed onto the tabletop. His heart rate set new records. Sabira had died there; Aneesa was born there and he recently met an angel in the courtyard. Since the conference room was dark, his reaction was hidden. He took a deep breath and asked to be excused.

He went to the men's room and leaned towards the mirror. His fingers were numbed by his quick shallow breaths. He stared at the beads of sweat assembling on his forehead. He splashed his face, wiped it dry, took a deep breath, and returned to the conference room. Brenda asked if he was OK.

"My mind exploded with endless possibilities. The excitement was overwhelming. That place has incredible potential. It's a dream, I love it!"

"Your interest and fervor is just what this project deserves and needs!" said Stoltz. "Today is Monday, let's not waste any time." Mr. Stoltz gave Ha-med a hearty hand shake, and continued, "Mr. Hassan, this project is all yours. Show us what you can do. Set up a meeting with McDaniel. Choose yourself a team. You'll need a draftsman, a runner with brains, and one of the students. Take some paper and stroll through the building. We don't have much time, in one week *you* present to the Hospital Board."

Ha-med dropped Aneesa off with her grandparents on Sunday with a suitcase of clothes and a box full of toys. He reviewed school times and meals, and asked Mrs. Ibrahim if she had any questions.

"She will be just fine, just go and do what you must. We'll see you next week." He lifted Aneesa, and gave her a hug. "I'll be just fine Dad, don't worry about me. Run off and do what you must!"

As he approached his car, an amazing sunset greeted him. There were flaming crimson streaks upon a cobalt panorama. As he gazed at the horizon, seagull's silhouettes joined in the dream-like twilight scene.

He stood, stared, squinted, and pondered. He had not been to the mosque in years; when Sabira died it lost its appeal. The project at hand and the glorious sky rekindled his interest.

As he approached to join his brothers for Maghrib, the full parking lot and crowded sanctuary surprised him. A guest was invited to join the group and following prayers, share his wisdom. Sheik Ahmed Muhammed Khalil was visiting from Palestine. The towering Sheik had a thick beard, a long flowing robe and a magnificent ancient Koran. His left hand was deformed and bore only three fingers. These fingers were twisted and bent and he had no fingertips. His thumb was flattened, but intact. At his sides sat two fierce-eyed young men. Young Muslims inspired by his writings poured into the hall.

"*Assalaam alaikum* my sheep." His voice shrieked and echoed, sending chills up Ha-med's spine. Throughout the speech, a dull constant roar of cheers made the walls tremble. He spoke of Islam being strangled by infidels. The effect of his wavering crippled left hand, and his right clutching an ancient Koran mesmerized the audience. He concluded with: "May Allah guard and protect us from non-believers."

Ha-med was terrified, but he did not know why. The sinister limo that drove through his village was lost long ago somewhere deep in his mind.

Mr. Ibrahim glowed when he noticed Ha-med.

Afridi startled him from behind. "Muhammed Hassan, it's been much too long!" After a cozy bear hug, he stood back, looked at Ha-med, and continued, "You look well. How have you been?"

The Imam walked over, also delighted to see Ha-med. "Muhammed Hassan, Allah has returned you to us on a special day. I'd like you to meet Sheik Khalil," said the Imam.

"Assalaam alaikum," said Ha-med.

"Wa alaikum Assalaam. Do you not attend the mosque regularly?" said the Sheik as he sized up Ha-med, and continued, "Do you not understand the importance community prayer?"

"Yes. But your message and meaning? Ana laa Afham! (I don't understand)!"said Ha-med.

In a salvage attempt, Afridi cut in. "So, Ha-med, tell us about your work. What fine structures are you building these days?" Ha-med spoke proudly of the Charles Cohen Clinic.

"Cohen?" said the Sheik. His inflamed eyes were in flames. "Does your company force you to work for those Jews and their Zionist Empire?" Ha-med's expression spoke louder than words.

"Have you ever visited Haifa?" said Ha-med.

"I will when *they* are all gone!"

Ha-med looked up at the Sheik, shook his head, turned his back and walked away.

Monday morning at four-thirty Ha-med prepared for his big day at bat. He knew that a Grand Slam was what he needed. He pulled up to the hospital where his team was waiting. Mike the draftsman: Brawny, brainy, and handsome. When not at work he was at the YMCA shooting hoops.

The second draft pick was from Brooklyn, New York. Phyllis M. Watts was an outstanding student. This pretty young black girl was number one in her class at Cornell. This architecture student had a minor in film.

The "gofer" everyone called Kris. His degree was in industrial design. Born in Kashmir, his name was Krishna Patel. He was a renaissance man, a jack-of-all-trades. If it existed, he could find it. If it didn't, he could build it. If he couldn't, he knew who could. He'd leave every morning on a scavenger hunt and return with whatever they needed. He'd negotiate traffic on bicycle or skateboard.

At 7 a.m., with a security escort, they toured the hospital building and its' grounds. Phyllis took pictures. Michael made sketches. Ha-med thought out loud with a Dictaphone in hand. Kris was scooting around town gathering archival information, old photos and blueprints.

They met in the hospital cafeteria for lunch. Across the room Ha-med spotted a familiar face entering the Doctor's Lounge. Marjorie Brennen stood there pregnant with an enormous smile aimed at Ha-med. He walked over and they greeted each other with smiles and hugs. Ha-med spoke of Aneesa and his job. Dr. Brennen had become the Obstetrics/Gynecology Residency Director, married a college professor, and had a two-year old son and a girl on the way. Ha-med told her about the plans to renovate the hospital. She was as excited as he.

"If there is anything I can do to help, let me know. It was a treat to see you Muhammed. Please hug and kiss Aneesa and her grandparents for me."

Kris returned with boxes of photos, plans, and old marketing stuff. The palatial appearance of the original building was magnificent. The cracking columns once were Athenian pillars, and the "graffiti wall" was an immense faux-granite slab. The actual property owned by the facility was twice the size of the land they utilized. The vacant lot had become overgrown with brush, weeds and trash. The dilapidated façade begged for their help. The ghosts came alive whispering stories of times before age took its' toll. The week soared by. They met on Friday with blueprints, photo enhancements, and a model Ha-med built. McDaniel made a rare appearance.

"So, let's see what you've got to show us," said McDaniel.

Ha-med pointed to the model and detailed it's components. The façade was re-plastered with neutral stucco, windows and doors trimmed with faux limestone. The once cracking columns were painted to resemble black granite. Spanning their tops were immense cedar posts and the old leaking roof was replaced with copper. The old cracking walkways became random flagstone slabs and above the grand entrance were glass angels in flight. Ha-med spoke of a park on the unused land. The Big Screen TV revealed computer enhancements of the interiors. Aqua and dark green floors, earth tone walls with walnut signage, and a sky-blue ceiling.

"Great job Ha-med," said McDaniel.

"You better get some rest, be refreshed. Today was easy. Monday at ten you meet on their turf," said Stoltz.

He flew over to Mahshi's where Aneesa was waiting. He hugged her and asked about her week. "School was fun, and me and my grandma did lots of stuff, I played the piano, and we had a good time. I only saw grandpa a couple of times he was always too busy to spend time with me.

Aneesa looked at her grandmother, then back at her father, "Can I take piano lessons?" She jumped on his lap. "Please daddy?"

"Do you think you are ready to practice piano every day, without getting bored?"

"I know I'm ready. I practiced all week. Grandma told me how good mommy was. Thanks dad. My first lesson is tomorrow a ten."

Grandma's proud smile glowed in the background. Ha-med proceeded to speak of his Cohen Clinic project. In mid-yawn Aneesa said: "I'm so proud of you daddy." She put up a fight, but her eyelids prevailed. Mr. Ibrahim was out at the Mosque for the evening.

"My husband said last week you joined them in prayer. Every one was so happy to see you. Momar mentioned that a wise Sheik was visiting."

"Do you know anything about the guest speaker? His philosophies or reputation?" asked Ha-med.

"I've heard he has written a great deal about the strife of our people, but my husband and I do not speak much of such things. What they say at the Mosque is between Allah and them."

They finished a snack and Mahshi's was empty. "Please check all the doors, and shut off all the lights," said Babi to the manager. She continued, "May Allah protect us tonight as we sleep."

They went back to the Ibrahim's. Momar was still out. They laid

Aneesa down on the couch. "So tell me my son, what goes on at the Mosque? Is there some deep dark secret hiding from me," said Mrs. Ibrahim.

"What else do you know of this visiting Sheik?"

"I know he is learned in Islamic Law, and has written a book called *Jihad Time.* He attracts the attention of young Muslims."

Ha-med was not sure what to say. They had always been open and honest with each other. "Our Prophet Muhammed spoke in his final sermon of how he demands we all live while on earth. *These words that I give you are not for one people. They were passed through the ages for all of mankind,*" said Ha-med.

"So, tell me. What is bothering you my son?" said Mrs. Ibrahim.

"What is your opinion of our non-Muslim brothers as bosses, employees, neighbors and friends?"

"It matters not how you choose to pray to our God, as long as you believe that Allah is the one, the only, the Supreme."

"I am concerned about the message the Sheik brings. He fills our youth with hate and fear," said Ha-med.

"Continue ... go on." As Ha-med was speaking, Mr. Ibrahim strolled into the room. "Good evening my wife, and my good son Muhammed." A blaring hush seemed to follow close behind. He continued, "Forgive my intrusion. Please, continue."

"It's getting late, I'd better head home," said Ha-med. "Since Aneesa is sleeping, and has piano in the morning, I'll leave her here if that's all right?"

"Of course," said Mrs. Ibrahim as the three of them watched her, all cuddled up on the couch. Ha-med lifted her, and moved her into the bedroom, as he said, "I look forward to meeting her piano teacher tomorrow. Where did you say you found her?"

"Mrs. Berger is new to this student, but not to this home or this piano ... Sabira was her star."

The next morning Ha-med went to pick up Aneesa. Her lesson was almost over. Mrs. Berger stepped away from the piano and whispered to Ha-med, "It is a pleasure to meet you. Your daughter is a most gifted child. Music flows through her veins." She paused, placed a hand on Ha-med's shoulder, and continued, "When I look into her eyes, I see her mother." They chatted a while, then Ha-med and Aneesa headed out for the day.

First to McDonald's, then to the park, and then to the mall for a carousel ride. They ended their day at movies with "Spy Kids" and stopped for pizza on the way home. By the time they got home, Aneesa was fast asleep. They pulled into the driveway. He looked at her face and thought of Sabira. He balanced Aneesa and reached for his keys. As he approached the door, he stood shocked in disgust. Black spray paint adorned his beige-creamy brick home. Staring at him, as high as the house was a huge black swastika next to a crescent moon with a star. Beneath it was a message, sloppily painted, "Arabs = Nazis." He placed Aneesa in his bed and called the police.

"We're are so sorry. There has been a rash of this stuff lately," said a police officer as they took fingerprints, photos and footprints.

"Do you have any paint here that matches your home?" asked one of the officers. Ha-med went to the shed and returned with a gallon and some brushes. In a matter of minutes the image was gone from the brick, but burned bright in his head. He thanked the officers and they left.

Ha-med lied by Aneesa, dozed off, and horrific memories haunted his dreams. He found himself lying in a tent on the stifling sand with his sister tugging on his leg. "Wake up. I'm hungry my brother and we've nothing to eat," she cried.

In a trembling sweat he awoke to Aneesa pulling at his leg.

"Get up sleepy head, let's get something to eat."

They went out for breakfast, then back to the Ibrahim's. He kissed her goodbye. She went straight to the piano, and played her scales as he walked out. Ha-med wasted no time. He drove to his office and practiced his presentation for hours.

On his way home Ha-med drove by the mosque. A mob was yelling. He pulled over. The stucco façades displayed billboards of hatred as spray-painted messages adorned its white walls. He stepped out and joined Afridi, the Imam, Mr. Ibrahim, and the Sheik. The visiting Sheik was out of control, bellowing and shrieking.

"It is now Jihad Time" and "Allah is great."

Ha-med stood tall and strong, and spoke in a loud suspicious voice of authority. He looked directly at the Sheik.

"This was the act of the few. Inciting a riot will reward their deeds." The crowd turned his way and he continued. "We don't want to reward them with this attention, that's exactly what they want us to do. Get brushes and buckets of paint. Let's erase hate from the walls, and gather in prayer. We are better than they."

The Sheik climbed up on top of his van, armed with a megaphone and yelled, "Death to them all! It is now Jihad Time. We must extinguish the flames before they spread and we burn. They will tear out our tongues with their stars and their crosses. Our voices they'll silence. They'll squash us like bugs."

His loud-screeching-magnified-horrific voice muted Ha-med's *a cappella* performance. The crowd started chanting to Sheik Khalil's lead: "Jihad Time" and "Allah is Great" ... "Jihad Time" ... "Allah is Great"

Police cars arrived with their microphones blasting: "It's time to go home now, your party is through." The Sheiks beady eyes pierced straight through Ha-med's soft soul. The crowds disbanded. Ha-med got into his Land Cruiser. As he started his car, he looked out his windows. On his left and his right were Sheik Khalil's two ghosts.

Just at that moment, a police car pulled up, and the phantoms disappeared. The policeman who helped him paint his home said to Ha-med: "Are you alright? Those two guys looked pretty scary. I heard your speech ... Ever considered politics?"

The next morning at eight Ha-med's alarm clock went off. His concentration was fogged by last night's events. He remembered dreaming, but not what he dreamt as he shaved, showered and sculpted his beard. He dressed in gray pants with a burgundy shirt and then slipped into a black blazer and admired the mirror. He felt Sabira was watching, and rooting for him.

He drove to the clinic and security escorted him to "The Kahane Educational Wing." A bronze wall was engraved with the names of the thousands who helped this old clinic survive. Henry Dominguez, the Hospital Administrator walked over and welcomed Ha-Med. "Mr. Hassan, you come well recommended, and I look forward to seeing your work. The Board of Directors is arriving. We've also invited a small group to critique your plans."

He shook Ha-med's hand, wished him good luck and led him up to the podium. Computer controls were at his hand on the console. Four-dozen spectators squeezed into the theatre. Ha-med scanned the room of mostly men in their sixties and a handful of women in fine silk or green scrubs. A tall man in the center looked right out of *The Chosen* and appeared ill at ease.

Mr. Dominguez walked up to the mic.

"Muhammed Hassan joins us today from the prestigious firm of McDaniel and Stoltz. His Masters degree with honors is from the Sorbonne. His reputation is stellar. Before we hand over the floor to our guest, I invite our board's chairman to say a few words. Would Ms. Carole Meyer please join me in welcoming our guest."

From the back of the room a woman stood up. Ha-med struggled to maintain his composure but her casual elegance set him ablaze. Her hair was brushed back to reveal her great eyes. Her business attire fit like a glove stopping short of her knees to expose her fine legs. When she approached him, their hearts each skipped a beat. This gorgeous dark man shyly sent her a smile. With a jerk of her head she sent one his way. She gave a well-prepared speech, thanked those who contributed, and honored her Grandfather. She then welcomed Muhammed Hassan.

To a round of applause, Ha-med shook Carole's hand and they stood in a dream. Ms. Meyer was flushed and was relieved when the lights dimmed. Ha-med took to the floor feeling crisp and alive.

"Good morning, and thank you for taking this time. We will show you our vision of how this Great Clinic should look." He thrilled them, entertained them, and took them from laughter to tears. Thanks to Kris's connections, they had files of photos, all retouched and enhanced. They dated back to the clinics birth, groundbreaking, and opening day. A breathtaking photo of the Cohen Clinic the day it first opened appeared on the screen. It remained in the background throughout the rest of the presentation. Then, a powerful image appeared in the foreground: The boys coming home from the Second World War. The Hospital wards filled with young broken bodies, teary-eyed girlfriends, and proud moms and dads. Newspaper headlines flashed, "We've Won the War!" Flags and parades ushered in better times.

Ha-med showed a series of great world achievements and dreadful disasters. The crash of the thirties, a nuclear mushroom, bombs based in Cuba, men on the moon, faces of Hitler, Einstein, the Beatles, President Kennedy, Kissinger, Nixon, Gorbechov and Gandhi. They flashed with a strobe-like effect. Throughout the photomontage, The Charles Cohen Clinic was always in view as it slowly decayed with the passage of time.

The screen faded to white, then a black and white photo appeared. No people, just the deteriorating building on a cold rainy day. Dismal, in need of repair.

Through computer animation, it morphed to the spectacle Ha-med designed. The landscape appeared to arise out of nowhere, lush lawns and a playground. The hospital building mended itself. Fresh stucco, slabs of stone, granite columns, huge cedar beams. The windows and doors became trimmed in limestone. The reflection of a brilliant blue sky bounced off the copper roof like a shinny new penny. The screen revealed a palatial fortress of wellness and health with glass angels in flight above the main entrance.

The scene dissolved to a garden where a young cherub sat perched on a bench. The camera closed in as Aneesa kneeled over. She stared at a stone that sat at her feet. Her voice floated on air as she read the inscription: "A Baby is God's Opinion That The World Should Go On."

The room lights were brightened to resounding applause. Mr. Dominguez thanked Ha-med, and announced that the model and photos were on display in the directors' lounge. The foyer was packed to the brim. Ha-med scanned the room for Carole. After a while, he gave up his search. Dr Brennen came over and in spite of her belly, gave him a bear hug and a kiss on his cheek.

"That was totally awesome, incredible. Congratulations."

When no one was watching she slipped something to him and whispered,"Put this in your pocket, hold on to it tight. Read it in private."

Ha-med kissed her cheek and his curiosity peaked. "Is it something important, should I take it and leave? Is it something I should go and look at right now?"

She smiled and thought to herself: "This is the Muhammed Hassan that I never met, so anxious and cute." She whispered to him: "Some more anticipation is just what you need. See ya 'round."

She disappeared back into the crowd. Off to his left he noticed the man with the black hat and strange sideburns immersed in a disagreement with several others. As Ha-med was leaving the tall man's sharp eyes were a crossbow with Ha-med aligned in its sights. His arrow of anger was a sharp blade of ice.

12

Decisions

Outside the clinic beneath a light drizzle the man's haunting gape lingered in Ha-med's mind. Had the Chassid mistook him for somebody else? The note in his pocket was buried beneath the lingering stare and the annoying rain. He quickened his pace and took cover under a canopy. When he reached for the keys out came the note. With his curiosity ignited, he clutched it and dashed to the car.

The repetitive heartbeat-like "*swoosh-click*" of the wipers caught Ha-med's attention, and the defroster's soft hush helped calm his nerves. The paper was carefully folded in eighths. The unfolding revealed a handwritten note ...

From the desk of
CAROLE MEYER

Dear Muhammed,
It is strange that I find myself writing this letter. Trust me when I tell you this is not my style. We don't know each other though some how I feel we have been friends for a very long time. Forgive my intrusion but I must confess that I pried into your life a few moments ago. I had to be sure there was no one to hurt, before I risked making a fool of myself!
I'd really enjoy it if we could just talk, with no preconceived notions of what will become. The few dates I have been on since my husband died were uncomfortable disas-

ters so I just gave it up. With Mother Teresa as my inspiration at first I considered becoming a nun. But since I am Jewish, it's just not an option, and besides that, it's too late. I have not been a saint!
If you find this letter the least bit enticing,
I'll be at the Manhasset duck pond on Sunday at noon.

-Carole

Ha-med read it twice over, and thought: "Had Sabira and Allah sent me a gift?" He looked up to the heavens for Allah's advice. The rain ceased. The sky cleared. A rainbow appeared. He read the letter again.

He drove down to his office and floated right in. Stoltz greeted him with "So, smiley, tell me about the presentation. How'd it go?"

"I think it went great. Tomorrow at ten the board meets. I don't know if I can stand the wait." A few moments later McDaniel arrived with Ha-med's team close behind.

"From the look on your face, I assume it went well. I guess somehow you misfits managed to pull it off. *Just kidding*. You've all worked your butts off. Get outa here. Take a day off. See ya Wednesday."

Stoltz, McDaniel, and Ha-med sat down for a chat. Stoltz broke the ice. "Our company has been growing steadily since day one. Now, for the first time, we've reached a plateau. We must choose a direction: up, or down. Down does not appeal to us. We've discussed options with our accountants."

McDaniel took over. "So, to make a long story short, we're heading to Wall Street and we'd like to take you along. You'll be given a seat on the Board and stock options along with your raise."

Ha-med hadn't recovered from Carole's smile or her letter, and now this. He was speechless, in shock, about to explode. He tried to say thanks, but his mouth wouldn't work. Stoltz bailed him out.

"You've thanked us enough. Take a day off. Say hello to Aneesa for us." After clutching their hands with a "*Thank you sir*" grip, he flew out the door and set out for a walk.

He strutted down Broadway with ping-ponging thoughts then

paused at the corner to let the crowds pass. He stood at the feet of New York's skyscrapers and these towers seemed fond of his euphoric grin. He browsed through a bookstore, chugged an espresso, took in some sites and got into his car.

First stop was Mahshi's to share the good news. He didn't know where to begin. The presentation, the raise, Wall Street. He chose not to mention Ms. Meyer just yet. He sat down for a snack, and gave all the details. Mrs. Ibrahim hugged him and Aneesa jumped into his arms. He grabbed his keys from his pocket, and didn't realize that Carole's note fell out. He gave Mrs. Ibrahim a hug and a kiss, put Aneesa on his shoulders, said good-bye and strolled out the door.

As he let Aneesa off his shoulders and unlocked the car, Mrs. Ibrahim yelled: "Ha-med, I think you dropped this." She was waving Carole's note at him. He walked back, and smiled with a rosy glow. He took the note, folded it, thanked her and he and Aneesa continued on their way. They stopped by the mall for pizza and ice cream. Aneesa was asleep before her ice cream was gone.

Ha-med woke up the next morning to a breakfast Aneesa had prepared. "Good morning kind sir, we sure hope you slept well. You and I sure do make a great team."

They dined, and they cleaned and he drove her to school. "See you later my angel." She hopped out from the car and blew him a kiss.

Back on Long Island the hospital board was just waking up in their Long Island homes. An accountant, two doctors, three lawyers, a diamond merchant, two bankers, and a man who owned furniture stores, all with big houses, big cars, big bank accounts and big egos.

Then there was Carole: *Chairman of the Board.* Honest, compulsive, good looking, and a fine-tuned fundraiser. Endearingly called "The Philanthropy Queen." Her Grandfather Charlie first started the clinic. Her Father and husband followed in Charlie's footsteps. The "Cohen-Meyer Foundation" provided Carole with a generous salary to help sooth the headaches of being so rich.

The hospital board had scheduled a meeting for ten a.m. At Nine forty-five fresh coffee, bagels and a fruit tray arrived. At nine-fifty five only Carole was there. An anxious lady with laptop, glasses on a strap around her neck, and a matronly outfit strolled in behind her.

"I'm here to record the minutes. Is this the right place? Did I get the dates mixed up?"

"They do this on purpose, just wait 'till your watch says five minutes past," said Carole.

At five after ten, all the others arrived and impatiently began the meeting.

"So, I'm sure we all know why we're here. Following last year's decision to renovate, checks have poured in. We interviewed over a dozen design groups. We've narrowed it down to three," said Carole.

Ms. Meyer handed out information packets and opened the floor to discussion. Several conflicting opinions fought for the floor. The accountant discussed how much over budget the project would likely go; the lawyer's concern was the contract, the doctor's problem was patient care when wards were closed and the furniture man had his own vested interest; the diamond man just stared at the rest.

Carole got fed up, slammed the gavel, and yelled. "Let's have some order. You're the ones in a hurry. I can stay all day."

A lawyer was given the floor.

"I brought an architect by last night to look over the plans and models. I trust his opinion; he's my father. He said that, hands down, the McDaniel and Stoltz proposal would win awards. None of the others even came close."

Carole struggled to restrain a huge sigh and a smile. Ha-med's patience, however, had taken the day off; anxiously, he glanced at his watch as he strolled around the vacant mosque.

Wandering into the Imam's empty office, he peered at the walls in amazement. A Master's in Theology from Yale. Undergraduate studies from Brown University. Art Major; rugby champ.

The Imam was a rare breed, a "born-again Muslim," born in New York, to Americanized parents. His father had been a high school math teacher, his mother had taught art. His grandparents had emigrated from Syria, and left their religion behind. During college, he'd discovered Islam and had followed Allah to his present profession.

The door startled Ha-med as the Imam entered.

"Good morning, Ha-med. So you took a day off? I'm honored that you chose to spend it with me."

Catching his breath, Ha-med returned the salutation.

"Imam, I recently delivered a major presentation."

"You mean the clinic improvements your company bid on that you impressed the entire board with yesterday?"

Ha-med was impressed, though not altogether surprised.

"Imam, may I seek your guidance in confidence?"

"Enlighten me with your disquiet. With direction from Allah we shall lighten your quandary."

"Well, Imam, tell me. What did you think of the Sheik's comments?"

"Muhammed Hassan, what did *you* think of the Sheik's comments?"

"Do you not think my approach was not more reasonable? Was my unsuccessful attempt to quell the storm not more appropriate than was his?" said Ha-med.

"In this case, my opinion is not the answer you seek. It is what *you* think, and what Allah thinks of what you think. Every problem has many right answers, and many wrong answers."

"Does the extremist philosophy not give rise to more hate, prejudice, intolerance?"

"Every religion – every philosophy – has extremists. Though regrettable indeed, their existence is crucial. They balance those who have flown far from the flock.

"To steady this scale is an infinite quest. To prevent it from tipping one way or the other is the challenge I face every day."

"But how can a man who claims to follow Allah still advocate violence against other men?" said Ha-med.

"They stand steadfast in their conviction that behavior is fated. No ally can convince them to sway this belief."

The Imam paused, placed a hand on Ha-med's shoulder, and continued, "In every religion these factions exist and until all others perish, we must maintain ours."

The Imam and Ha-med just left it at that. They shook hands, smiled and a renewed bond was formed. Ha-med drove into the city.

Still seeking a break from his exhausting week, Ha-med caught a matinee of *The Girl on the Bridge*. Back in France he'd loved action/adventure, but now he had a taste for those arty French films. From the phone in the lobby he called up his boss.

"Mr. Stoltz, has anyone heard, have they made a decision?"

"I thought I told you to take the day off? No, Ha-med. Now go take a break, and call me at three."

When the theatre was dimmed, it struck Ha-med that the Sheik and Chassid shared the same look of rage.

"What could have caused these religious men to harbor such anguish?"

Then the monochrome scene on the bridge caught Ha-med's attention. The leading lady was preparing to jump.

The story hooked him and reeled him in. For two hours, he was gone.

The hospital board continued to praise Ha-med's project.

"I also favored that design, but what do I know of such things?" said Carole.

"It seems that the proposal from McDaniel and Stoltz has been nominated. Do I hear a second?" said the accountant.

As the furniture salesman was about to second the motion, Kahane's face reddened.

His fist struck the table with a resounding thump. He rose to his feet. His sleeves were rolled up revealing on his forearm the faded green numbers, a permanent reminder of a youth he never had.

His voice screeched like a braking locomotive.

"This clinic we speak of is The Charles *Cohen* Clinic, the educational addition is the *Kahane* wing. Dr. *Meyer* generously renovated the surgical suites. I forbid you to hire some filthy young Arab. Not one morsel of work for them. Not one. I will not let that happen. Never!"

The group was shocked at this emotional explosion. Mr. Kahane's unyielding stance silenced the room. They disagreed, yet not one would challenge him.

Carole had never seen Mr. Kahane like this. She stood up and spoke like the toughest teacher in an inner city ghetto school.

"Mr. Kahane, sit down now or leave the room. We've heard your opinion. I open the floor for a productive discussion. Does anyone care to comment constructively?"

The smoke in the room settled. Fuming, Mr. Kahane chose to sit down.

"On the one hand, I can appreciate Mr. Kahane's point. In Israel, more bombings occur every day," said the accountant who paused, and then continued with a tremolo. "On the other hand I feel that regarding our project, our only concern is who will do the best job at the best price."

The furniture merchant rose.

"In the business community, reward is by merit. The presentation and design by Muhammed Hassan was the best. I'd be ashamed to deny him the contract based on his religion!"

Mr. Kahane stood tall once again. He crashed his fist down even louder this time.

"Your naïve remarks insult me. You speak of shame? Do *they* know of shame when they're bombing our schools? You speak of reward? Payments and parades when *they* blow up our shops?"

Kahane looked faint, pale. He perspired and trembled as he reached for a glass of water. His nerves were shot. The glass was shaking. He sat down.

Carole stood up and surveyed the group.

"You have until Friday. Think long and think hard."

Behind her was a shelf with some books, paper, and assorted office supplies. She found a tin half-full with old, stale sugar cookies, and passed them out, each accompanied by a slip of paper.

"We will vote by closed ballot. The majority will rule. The decision will stand."

"These are your ballots," she said. "After you've cast your vote, place the ballots in this tin, which will be at the security entrance. Friday at 10, I will tally the votes. The meeting is now adjourned!"

Kahane was determined to get the last word in. He stormed out yelling and clutching his chest: "How can you support those blood-sucking Arabs?"

The matinee was just what Ha-med needed. As his eyes adjusted to the daylight, he looked at his watch, and it was almost three. He drove to his office and walked up to Mr. Stoltz. "So, what have we heard?"

"I just got off the phone with Mr. Dominguez. They won't make their decision until Friday morning, so until then we need to be patient and wait."

Ha-med hid his disappointment beneath a veil of optimism.

"I guess we'll just wait till the fat lady sings."

"One tune from me and you'll regret that cliché." said Brenda.

The endless workweek crept by.

On Friday morning, Aneesa said, "Daddy, you look so intense. Please smile for me ... what does *intense* mean?"

He drove her to school, gave her a kiss and a hug.

"You're just like your mother."

She smiled and thanked him as she ran off to join her classmates.

He got to the office at nine o'clock sharp. He found concentration nearly impossible as he stared at the clock.

Ms. Meyer strolled to security, grabbed her tin, paced to her office, and closed the door. She sat at her desk, gazed at the box, and then toward the heavens while crossing her fingers.

She grasped one vote at a time between her right thumb and index finger, slowly unfolded it and set it neatly on the desk.

Those for McDaniel and Stoltz were placed on her right, and all other votes would be placed on her left.

There were no other votes. Nine board members had cast votes. Three had abstained.

It was unanimous: McDaniel and Stoltz.

In her mind were two faces: Kahane's and Ha-med's.

She had known Kahane since childhood. He was kind, and wise and had always treated her well. He was family. The thought of his face as he pounded the table gave her chills, yet she regretted the way she'd spoken to him. What would her grandfather have said, had he been there?

At the same time, her attraction to Ha-med was undeniable, though she didn't even know him. The thought of his shy smile gave her goose bumps.

She phoned the board members and shared the results.

No one who had abstained would admit to having done so. With trepidation she called Kahane's office. Carole knew that Friday was his favorite day of the week; Sabbath was his day dedicated to God with all the mysticism and ritual that it entails.

He would stop work at noon, get his hair cut, pick up his suit from the cleaners, stop by the bakery and then swing by the liquor store on his way home.

When Carole was young, her grandfather and Kahane would frequently welcome the Sabbath together, humming Yiddish melodies, setting up the candles; and impatiently wait for the sun to set.

After several rings, "Kahane's, may I help you?" said Maurice, the warehouse manager.

"Hi Maurice. Good Shabbas. This is Carole Meyer. May I speak with Mr. Kahane?"

Silence preceded his answer. "*Gotteniu*! Carole, have you not heard? Mr. Kahane is at Mount Sinai ... He had a heart attack on Monday afternoon ... on his way home from the board meeting."

"Oh God! I didn't know."

Carole felt her own heart pounding. It felt to her as if her heart were trying to work its way out of her chest. She shook with fear, guilt, remorse, but most of all, worry. With her voice shaking, and eyes tearing, she continued, "He's going to be all right, isn't he?"

She mopped her eyes, blew her nose, and continued, "Please tell me he's going to be all right."

"He was transferred out of the ICU this morning. He's doing a little better."

"How come no one called me?"

"Mr. Kahane wanted it that way. He's kept it real quiet. Only a few know about it. The Rabbi has been with him all week."

"Thanks," said Carole as she hung up the phone. It was ten thirty in the morning. Rush hour just ended and the lunch rush had not yet begun so the traffic was light on the Long Island Expressway. She stopped by her house, and picked up a picture. It was Carole at age four in Kahane's arms. She drove into the city. Her late husband's parking sticker let her enter the doctor's lot. She stopped by the nursing station, and asked for the charge nurse.

"What room is Mr. Kahane in?" said Carole.

"I'm sorry. He is not accepting visitors. If you care to leave your name, I will let him know you stopped by," said the nurse.

"Can you tell me how he is doing?" said Carole.

"Well, we are not permitted to give out patient information, but he was transferred out of the ICU this morning, and that's a good sign. The doctor said his heart attack was mild."

"Thank you so much," Carole handed her an envelop with the photograph inside, and continued, "Would you please give this to him, and let him know that Carole Meyer stopped by."

"Oh, I'm so sorry. Are you Mrs. Meyer?"

The nurse stood up, took Carole's hand, and continued, "It is so nice to meet you. We all miss Dr. Meyer so much around here. Mr. Kahane's in room 553, end of the hall on the right."

Carole wasn't sure if she was relieved or not. She walked over and tapped on the door. A man opened it, a familiar face. It was Rabbi Goldberg. He shook Carole's hand, and she whispered, "Rabbi, how is he today?"

"A *bisel* better, thanks be to God!" said the Rabbi.

"I'm not deaf, and I'm not dead. Who is it, Rabbi?" said Kahane. Carole walked in, and Kahane spoke before she could manage to squeeze in a word.

"Hello Carole. I'm glad you're here."

He paused, sipped on some water, and continued.

"I've known you for half my life, and your whole life. Your judgment has always impressed me. You are as stubborn as your mother, articulate as your father and dogmatic as your grandfather. What am I going to do with you?"

Carole was relieved by his tone, and stuttered with sniffles and tears.

"I am so sorry. I showed such disrespect. I had no right!" said Carole, as Kahane cut her off again.

"*Sha, Maidle.* I deserved it. You know, it's funny. When I left the meeting on Monday, I think God was telling me something ... or was he reminding me of something I had long ago forgotten? Ethics of our Fathers tells us that: *A hot-tempered person cannot teach.* Your grandfather would be proud. I'm proud. You stood up. You spoke your mind. You were the only *man* in the room. *Mazel Tov.*"

"Ha-med ... I mean McDaniel and Stoltz will make us proud. You will see. Good *Shabbas,* Mr. Kahane," said Carole, as she handed him the envelope.

"*Vos iz dos*?" said Kahane. He took out the picture, and smiled with tears. Good *Shabbas,* Carole. Take care. Be a good girl."

"Rest. Feel better. *Zei gezunt*," said Carole as she kissed his forehead.

"*A braireh hob ich*? (I have a choice?)"

Carole went down to her car, and on her cellular phone, she called McDaniel and Stoltz. "This is Carole Meyer, may I please speak with Mr. McDaniel?"

"He is out of the office. May I take a message?" said Brenda.

"May I speak with Mr. Stoltz?"

They are both out of the office. Perhaps Mr. Hassan can assist you today ... Hello? Are you still there, dearie?" said Brenda, thinking they had gotten cut off.

"Yes, that would be fine. I will speak with Mr. Hassan."

She put Carole on hold. Carole did not know if Ha-med planned to show up on Sunday, or not. She didn't even know for sure if he had read the note, and if he had, she did not know if he thought it was appropriate. She was nervous as a teen sitting by the phone hopping that some guy she had a crush on would call to ask her out.

"Ha-med, this is Brenda. Ms. Carole Meyer is calling, should I put her through? ... Hello? Ha-med? ... Are you there?"

After a silence, Ha-med said, "Yes, give me a minute."

He cleared his throat and continued, "Please put Ms. Meyer through."

"Good morning, Ms. Meyer. This is Mr. Hassan. How are you today?"

"I'm doing quite well, thank you, and I have some good news."

"Tell me we got the job."

"Yep, we, I mean you got it. Please have someone arrange for the contracts to be signed. The board is looking forward to a festive groundbreaking celebration. It was nice to speak with you again."

Before she hung up, she said: "If there will be nothing else ... "

Ha-med interrupted.

"Yes, Ms. Meyer, there is just one more item I wish to review with you now if I could … Would it be alright with you if on Sunday I brought my Aneesa to join us at the duck pond at noon?"

Carole was glad she was all alone. She took a mirror from her purse and delighted in her own child-like grin of relief.

"Certainly Mr. Hassan. That would be just fine. I look forward to seeing both of you on Sunday."

Ha-med caressed the phone as if Carole was inside it. He struggled to compose himself, and he walked up to Brenda.

"We got it – we got the contract!"

Brenda was not the least bit surprised, though she shared Ha-med's exhilaration.

"I'm so happy for you."

She stood up and gave him a hug and then smiled and said with a wink, "Just tell me one thing, Mr. Muhammed Hassan, how come that short, quick simple message took such a long time to deliver and receive?"

13

Memory

Memory: Alas but a double-edged sword.
Past? Present? Future? An amalgam of time.
Poisonous tragedies obstruct your potential,
Snakes from your history choke you to death.
Roll with the punches, no matter how venomous.
The antidote? Rise up. Be better than they.

A. The Chassid

Mr. Kahane was a marvelous man, respected by many, and feared by the rest. When his family fortune had been seized by the Nazi's, his father had resisted and was hanged in his home.

At age 12, he'd assisted the infants at Auschwitz, and many survivors still owed him their lives. For the crime he committed of being born Jewish, they'd tortured him so he could not reproduce.

His stunning mother had been spared for a while. When she had become pregnant, and no longer a playtoy, her body had been used for their experiments. Like a lab rat they'd examined her fetus and then discarded her body as medical waste.

Upon camp liberation, he had nowhere to go, but miraculously he'd managed to find his way home.

His childhood dreams, along with his mansion, were shattered and empty and haunted by ghosts.

He knew there was a cigar box hidden beneath the floorboards, tightly secured in a sealed plastic bag.

Uncertain of its contents, he reached down and grabbed it. He stuffed it in a sack full of clothing and food, and stowed away his thin body on a ship to New York.

Upon his arrival he looked in the box teeming with twinkling stars. He froze, eyes opened wide. Even at 14, he appreciated the value of a box packed with glittering stones. He bound it with tape to his skinny frail chest. He was taller than average so his lean slender body provided safe haven beneath baggy shirts.

He lived for a while on Delancy Street handouts, where the Chassidic Jews took a liking to him. He was taken in and adopted by a pious young Rabbi, who shared his guidance and teachings with the boy.

On his eighteenth birthday, he revealed to his new father the boxful of diamonds he'd hid for four years.

With the Rabbi's assistance they started a business and together they prospered. A decade passed by and their jewelry-store chain became shopping mall fixtures all over the world.

In honor of his murdered parents, he planted a forest on Israeli soil. In 1973, he decided to go pay his forest a visit and checked in to a luxury suite at the King David Hotel.

He enjoyed Rosh Hashanah like never before, and he felt that his new life had finally begun. The week flew by. He woke up on Yom Kippur morning. His fasting had started the night before and he tried to forgive those less pious than he.

Instead of reflection, repentance, and memorial prayers, he was greeted by gunfire and deafening blasts.

On Israel's holiest day, this small struggling country was attacked by 1,400 Syrian tanks, and 80,000 Egyptian soldiers. Soon after, 18,000 Iraqis, 3,000 Saudis, and 2,500 Moroccans aided by Libyan fighter jets, Lebanese radars, and Jordanian tanks eagerly joined in. This act of aggression was another failed effort to kill all the Jews. When will *they* learn?

With God's Almighty hand, and His strong outstretched arm, David defeated Goliath again. The offending armies were forced to retreat while the Jewish experienced déjà vu and thought "Never Again!"

Before this had happened, Kahane had been happy just hating the

Nazis for what they had done. After this traumatic turn of events, he hated the Arabs with equal distain.

B. The Sheik

Today, there is a village in the Middle East where orchards produce oranges larger than grapefruits and shade trees provide shelter from the sweltering sun. Half a century ago it was an infertile desert, where Muslims had lived for centuries. They tended their goats, prayed to Allah, and were content with their lives under British control.

On a cool winter evening, a caravan passing through set up camp for the night. The villagers and visitors huddled around a fire, roasting a goat while a handsome young sultan sang songs and told tales. A young woman was smitten. When the caravan parted her sultan remained and these soul mates soon married and planted a seed.

One sunrise the sultan joined his brothers in prayer. As they bowed and faced Mecca, they were ambushed by an ax-wielding Zionist terrorist gang.

They were viciously butchered. All that remained from the soul of her sultan was his life-bearing seed and his sacred Koran.

In the heat of the summer a child was born. His mother would spend hours reading him the Koran and her comforting arms would be his only refuge.

By the time he turned five, this gifted child could read forwards and backwards with equal finesse. He spoke Arabic like a sultan, Hebrew like a rabbi and English like a noble from a fine British school. He held his Koran in two sacred places: in his long-fingered hands and entrenched in his mind.

On a cold winter morning the child was sleeping. British Rule had ceased and a battle ensued. His small peaceful village was woken by loud smoke-spewing monsters with death in their lifeless eyes. He watched as these demons devoured their goats, and saw blue Stars of David invade his small town. He ran toward his mother but he was too late. Her body was crushed beneath gargantuan, mechanized feet.

Those who know the story continue to wonder, "Why did *they* not accept the partition plan?" Most lives that were lost were "collateral damage," innocents unaware of what hit them, or why.

As Ahmed lay clinging to life in a pile of death, a jeep of sad farmers paused, prayed, and drove on. The last sight he saw as they ran over his hand was the echoing image of a six-cornered star. This crippled, penniless prodigy orphan wandered for weeks clutching his sacred Koran in his only good hand.

A group of young Arabs with machine guns in hand, hatred in heart and "Jihad" in their heads approached an old hut. They heard heated debating in both Arabic and Hebrew, and a soft-spoken Brit tried to comment, but failed. With vigilance and guns drawn they entered the hut. They rummaged around but found only a boy. A majestic Koran was in his right hand, and his left hand held maggots and dry caked-on blood.

They took the boy in as a gift from Allah. They had dark, unkempt beards and long flowing turbans and opposed any Israel regardless of cost. He followed their example and became their salvation. First he followed them but soon they followed him.

14

The Picnic

Crimson silhouettes of autumn leafed trees tapped Ha-med's window, "It's time to wake up."

He squinted and yawned then noticed Aneesa was standing there dressed at 8:23. She was ready and raring to go. She nudged him.

"Wake up, sleepy head. It's so pretty outside. Let's go have some fun."

"Hey, I've got an idea. How would you like to go for a picnic?" Before Ha-med had time to finish his thoughts, Aneesa was at the door.

"First, I need to jump in the shower. Then you and I will go buy us some food," said Ha-med.

Aneesa gathered the ice chest, fetched a basket and impatiently paced. Ha-med could think of nothing but Carole. He jumped in the shower thinking of her thick wavy hair and her slender, shapely body. Her sultry smile was etched in his mind. He dried himself off, chose soft silky slacks and a snug-fitting sweater. He picked up the phone and dialed Haifa. The sound of Shaina's "Shalom" was a great way to start his day. Ha-med spoke of his success at work, and then spoke of what really excited him.

"I've met a women. She's a widow, we barely know each other, but I feel I've known her for a thousand years. It's that chemistry thing, we seem to just click, ya know what I mean?"

"I'm so happy for you. She's one lucky girl!" said Shaina.

Yoav picked up the phone: "Mazel Tov. You deserve to meet someone. Just be sure to follow your heart, not your hormones."

Aneesa and her dad drove off to the market for whole-wheat bread, sliced turkey, mustard, mayo and some coleslaw and cold juices. For the "*piece de resistance*" they grabbed a fresh apple pie. The princess climbed up on her grocery-filled chariot as her father, the King, fueled her carriage. They climbed into the car at a quarter to twelve.

"Boy, I sure have a good-looking dad."

"And I have the cutest little daughter in the entire world."

"Daddy, where are we going for our picnic?"

"How 'bout we share our bread with some ducks at a park?"

They pulled up to the curb, she hauled the basket, he dragged the ice chest and they strolled hand-in-hand on a glorious day. Their approach toward the pond was interrupted when Aneesa noticed a woman sitting all alone on a bench.

She was shimmering. The sun's rays peaked through the tree's wavering branches, bounced off the pond and sent intermittent flickering sparks off Carole's dark glasses. From Carole's vantage point, the sun silhouetted Ha-med's and Aneesa's approach like a scene from some classic black-and-white film. Carole squinted and used her hand as a visor.

"Daddy, Daddy, look! It's that pretty lady I met at the hospital. Can we go say hello to her? Can we?" Her father said yes, and they walked up to Carole.

"Hello Ma'am. Do you remember me?"

"I most certainly do. Isn't your name Aneesa? Last time we spoke you wore a rose-colored dress."

"Carole, do you remember my father? His name is Ha-med."

Carole lifted her shades and smiled at Ha-med. She and Ha-med spoke in synchronized harmony, "It's so nice to see you again."

The three of them giggled. Aneesa tugged at her father and he bent down.

"Can we invite Carole to join us for lunch?"

"Ms. Meyer, is it? My daughter and I were about to have a picnic. Would you care to join us?"

"I would be honored to dine with such distinguished hosts, but I give you fair warning: I eat like a horse!"

They laughed while surveying the park. They sought a shady spot near the pond with some soft ground to sit on. They found just the spot, beneath a century-old oak twenty feet from the ducks.

They set up a blanket and sat themselves down. A beautiful woman, a man and a child with green grass, a blue sky and ducks in the pond. The reflection of orange and brown on the trees mimicked the highlights of Carole's hair. If Monet had been there with canvas and paints he could not have improved on this glorious scene.

The three sat and talked about school, work, and life and Aneesa got bored. "Daddy, can I go feed the ducks now?"

"Sure, but be careful. And please don't go in the water."

Ha-med and Carole shared heart-wrenching tales of their lives plagued with sorrowful untimely death. When they realized their spouses died on the very same day their minds embraced. Their bodies craved to do the same.

At last, their hearts felt they could love again. Their slow, soft deep breaths gave their voices a rest. They inched closer together but dared not touch, as Aneesa stood smiling at the ducks, and back at them.

Aneesa returned and sat down between them. They devoured huge turkey sandwiches, gulped down the juice and then polished off the apple pie.

As Aneesa was falling asleep, Carole began tidying up. She gathered the trash, arranged the utensils, folded the napkins, and placed their belongings in the basket. Ha-med watched her every move. He recalled the perfect penmanship on the neatly folded note. He smiled as he watched her seemingly perpetual motion.

"Do you ever just sit back, relax and take in the sights?" said Ha-med.

Carole blushed as Ha-med leaned back against the old tree. His cherub was sound asleep with her head on his knee. Carole moved closer and leaned her head on his chest. He gently proceeded to caress her neck. Her eyes closed.

Ha-med made sure his Aneesa still slept as he placed his warm lips behind Carole's ear.

"I think I am falling in love," he whispered.

These words filled her body and soul with desire, as she had craved for so long to again hear these words. Eyes tightly closed, she hoped to soon taste his lips as she moistened her own with the tip of her tongue.

He moved his warm lips from her neck to her mouth. She could sense her nipples becoming erect. Teased by her tongue, she spread her lips wide and like two high school virgins they embraced deeply.

They tenderly parted their lips, as their eyes remained closed and their hearts opened wide. When their synchronized breathing and beating hearts settled, they opened their eyes and shared a sigh. Their pulsating veins flowed with erotic thoughts.

They had both endured more than their fair share: broken hearts, broken lives, shattered dreams, feeling lost. It was time to get on with their lives. They stared at the angel upon daddy's knee. She stretched, yawned, looked up and smiled. The three of them laid in a row on their backs and looked at downy white clouds on a pastel blue sky.

"Look over there," Carole pointed. "I see a camel with one big hump on his back."

"I see it too, I see it," said Aneesa.

"I see a man with a big white beard," said Ha-med.

"I see it! Look over there, I see a big fluffy heart," said Aneesa.

"That's my heart, and look how it's throbbing," said Carole

"I see a soft comfortable bed," said Ha-med.

Aneesa used her hand as a visor and squinted, trying to see it, then gave up, stood up, and signaled the others to join her. She took a hand from her father, and one from Ms. Meyer, and she ran, jumped, and swung clutching onto their hands. She let their hands go and she went skipping and spinning. She danced and she laughed more than ever before. She stopped and faced them, and then looked straight at Carole.

"How would your sons like a sweet little sister like me?"

Carole knelt down and took Aneesa's hand.

"Well, since you are so cute, so much fun to play with and so well behaved, I'm sure they would just love to meet you. And when they do, I think you should just ask them yourself."

"Thanks, that's exactly what I'll do!"

They packed up their stuff and walked Carole to her car. When Aneesa saw the shiny green convertible Jaguar XKR, she said, "Wow, that's so cool. Can I go for a ride?" She looked up at her father. "Oh, Please, Daddy, please can I?"

"You'll have to ask Carole."

May I please have a ride in your car? Pretty please?"

Since the car had only two seats, Ha-med knew he'd be taking a walk. Aneesa and Carole hopped into the car, fastened their seatbelts and off they went. Carole's eyes were fixed on the road; Aneesa's eyes were fixed on Carole.

Even at five, she admired Carole's beauty. This was the first time in Aneesa's short life that she wondered what having a mother must be like. Carole detected her curiosity.

"So, tell me what you are thinking, my little friend."

"This car is so cool. When I'm older will you teach me to drive?"

"That you can bet on."

"What are your kids' names? What do they do?"

"They are both away in college. David is the serious type. He's at Yale University, wants to be a great surgeon some day. Andy loves to have fun. He is a very talented musician. He attends Eastman School of Music. When they come home to visit, would you like to meet them?"

"Don't you remember? I'm going to meet them and ask them if they want a little sister."

They found Ha-med perched on the hood of his SUV. He jumped down and walked up to their window. Using a handshake as their excuse, he and Carole held hands. He started to lean closer, but as Carole's lips approached, they hesitated, content to part instead with broad smiles.

15

Grandmas' Advice

Ha-med awoke Monday morning at six with the sweet taste of Carole's warm lips on his mind. His euphoric mood and Aneesa's bright smile were more than enough to jump-start his day.

"What do you say we go out for breakfast before I drop you off at school?"

They drove to a diner and sat in a booth and ate as they spoke of their new friend. He gave her a kiss as he dropped her at school.

"See you tonight," he said as she hugged him goodbye.

He drove to the city and as he was parking, McDaniel and Stoltz were arriving as well. The three of them rode up together on the elevator. By the time they arrived on their floor, many details of project "M1263" had been discussed and decided. They grabbed their coffee and headed over to the conference room where Brenda and the rest of the team were rolling out blueprints and viewing the model. Stoltz gave a pep talk.

When he finished, McDaniel said: "One week from today we break ground. Then we have eighteen months to finish the job. The time will fly by."

"Ha-med, this one's all yours, so have at it," said Stoltz.

"So, Mr. Hassan, are your ready for your big break? Do you think you can handle this one, and really run the show?" asked McDaniel.

Ha-med was careful not to sound overconfident. He was a little suspicious of McDaniel's tone, as if it was a trick question. He'd been with the firm for a decade, and they know his potential and expertise.

Then McDaniel directed a question to Stoltz.

"So, when are you going to let him in on *your* little surprise? Or, should I tell him?"

Now Ha-med was really on edge. Stoltz took the floor. "It's been years since my wife and I have been on a real vacation. We've been talkin' about it for months. Well Ha-med, do you think you are ready to start this one without me breathing down your back? I'm leaving in a few days, and we'll be gone, out of touch, for three months."

Ha-med was honored and excited. This was the first project of such magnitude he would handle without Stoltz at his side. Not only could he prove himself, he would also have the opportunity to work closely with Carole.

Aneesa's school day zoomed by, and she awaited grandma's arrival.

"Good afternoon, my little angel. How was your day?" said Grandma.

"It was great! We learned all about trees. Did you know that they can take water from the ground and move it hundreds of feet up their trunks? My teacher says no one can figure that out. I think it's a secret that Allah has chosen to keep between himself and his trees."

"And tell me my little Aneesa, how did you and your father spend a beautiful Sunday afternoon?"

Aneesa lit up like the Fourth of July.

"You would have loved it, Grandma. We had a picnic at a park with ducks and we met a nice lady who remembered my name, so I asked her to join me and Daddy for lunch and she did. We had so much fun." As Aneesa proceeded to talk of the picnic, grandma's curiosity ballooned; it was ready to burst.

"After lunch she took me for a ride in her cool sports car and told me about her sons Andrew and David. They're away at college. David's at Yale, Andrew's at Eastman. I think she misses them. She has no husband. She must be lonely."

As Mrs. Ibrahim parked in front of Mahshi's, she asked, "And what is the name of this nice new friend of yours, and your dad?"

"Her name is Ms. Meyer, but I call her Carole, and so does daddy. She's really nice. You will just love her."

"I hope I get to meet her very soon, but for now let's not concern your grandfather with new friends. That way we can surprise him after

I've met your friend Carole."

That evening when Ha-med went by to pick up Aneesa, Mr. Ibrahim was at the mosque and Aneesa was immersed in the piano. Her eyes were closed and her head swayed with emotion. A Chopin prelude, Opus 28 No. 4, was simplified so her little fingers could play the left hand. She didn't even hear her father sneak in as he tiptoed over and joined Mrs. Ibrahim on the couch.

"She just finished her scales, and will continue to practice for about forty-five minutes," said Mrs. Ibrahim. "Are you hungry? I have some grilled chicken with raisins." They slipped into the kitchen while Aneesa played on.

"So tell me, my son. Aneesa spoke fondly of a Ms. Meyer. I have not before heard mention of her name, though I do confess that I saw it on the note she sent you. This Carole, is there something to her?"

He loved Mrs. Ibrahim like a mother. After contemplating how to best proceed, he let his heart speak. "Not too long ago Aneesa and I went to relax in the enclosed courtyard at the Cohen Clinic. This is where we first encountered Carole. We spoke briefly then parted. When I went to the clinic to present my proposal, our paths crossed again. It turns out she is the Chairman of the Board, and her grandfather was Dr. Cohen. I could not get her off my mind. We made plans to meet for a Sunday afternoon picnic. A meeting that Aneesa thought was a coincidence. As our conversation deepened, we realized that our spouses passed on, on the very same day. I'm not sure who loves her more, Aneesa or I. Could Allah have planned this?"

Mrs. Ibrahim stood up, placed her hands on his temples, kissed his forehead and spoke.

"Your life has been challenged from every perspective. You deserve to love again, and if Carole is the one, it will be with my blessing. Heed my advice my son. While Allah watches over and grants his approval, some Hebrews and Muslims will think you two a disgrace. Your minds now are blinded by love's sweet caress. Make certain you're willing to combat love's threats."

Ha-med hugged her, and thanked her.

"I know you will love her." said Ha-med.

After a snack, Ha-med and Aneesa went home.

On Wednesday afternoon, Ha-med got out of work a little early and Aneesa was at Grandma's house. Three days had passed since the day at the park. Ha-med drove home and went straight to the phone and dialed Carole's number. After several rings, he got a recording.

"You have reached the Meyer residence. Please leave a brief message and your number. We will get back to you as soon as we can. Thank you."

Ha-med's day was brighter just hearing her voice. He left her a message. "Dear Carole, this is Ha-med. Just got in from work. I'm going to pick up Aneesa. I'll try you again later ... You are all I think about."

The Long Island Expressway was always jam-packed, but traffic was even worse then usual. As the creeping flow inched a bit further, he saw flashing red lights, police cars and an ambulance. One car was flipped over; another one crushed. A woman was placed on a stretcher; a man on the ground gushed blood from his scalp. Another with a Bible recited a verse to death's silhouetted contour beneath a white sheet.

Ha-med's mind flashed back to Sabira lying in the morgue. He took a deep breath with his eyes closed. He opened them, wiped them off, and sluggishly drove on. His hunger to share Carole's warmth grew.

He arrived at the Ibrahim's shaken though pensive. He relayed the experience to Mrs. Ibrahim, then he and Aneesa headed on home. As they pulled into the driveway, the phone started ringing. Too tired to hurry, they let it ring.

Carole's long day was equally exhausting. Her daily routine was an ongoing saga of sharing her wealth with less fortunate folks.

Just before sunrise she imagined Ha-med whispering, "I think I am falling in love." With passionate thoughts of the warmth of his lips, her body surrendered to her curious fingers.

With a satisfied smile, she got out of bed, and slipped into the shower. Over breakfast she reviewed the appeals for the day. Photos of sickness and words of despair attempted to persuade her to fund their requests. She finished breakfast then ran off to the gym. By nine she was ready to listen to those who tried to convince her to donate some funds. A group raising money for AIDS, another for abused children and rape victims. She stopped at a theatre where first-rate musicians could no longer play since they'd run out of funds. Her last appointment was at a halfway house established by her father to house the homeless and help them find work.

On her way home she stopped by the clinic and admired the scaffolding surrounding its walls. She remembered how awesome it had looked when she was a child. She would prance through the hallways as proud as could be, in a miniature white lab coat at grandfather's side.

Her Jaguar purred into her circular drive as the cool, tranquil sunset welcomed her home. Under the soothing cover of October skies, she opened the roof, leaned her head back and admired her view.

She strolled into her kitchen, opened the fridge, poured some white wine and then retired to her bedroom. The light on her answering machine was flashing away. She reached over to the side table, pushed the button, sat up on the edge of her bed, and listened to a long string of messages separated by annoying beeps.

"Hey Mom, are you making a turkey next month? Gimme a call."

-Beep

"If this is Ms. Carole Meyer, would you join us next Thursday for our Annual Hadassah Fundraiser Meeting? Your input is always helpful."

- Beep

"Hi Mom, this is Andrew, I miss you. Where are you? I'm doing well. On weekends I'm playing in a country-rock band. Oh, yeah, by the way, I met this girl ... she has no Thanksgiving plans. So get back to me if we have room in our quaint humble home to accommodate one more. She's little, doesn't eat much."

A beep then passed by with no message at all, and the next one offered her a new credit card, followed by a recorded sales pitch from a long-distance telephone service. Then came the voice she was longing to hear. Her legs dangled over the edge of the bed; she reclined, extending her arms out to her sides.

"Dear Carole, this is Ha-med. Just got in from work. I'm goin' to pick up Aneesa. I'll try you again later. You are all I think about."

She played it again, then again with her eyes closed. She dialed his number and got a recording. "You have reached me and my Daddy, we can't come to the phone. Please leave us a message so we know who you are so we can decide if we want to call you back or not."

Carole laughed out loud, rolled over onto her belly, and left a message. "Aneesa and Ha-med it is now 6:30, I was hoping to catch you before it got to late, so when … "

Aneesa sat on her father's shoulders; they grabbed the mail, and strolled up the walkway. She jumped down and unlocked the door. As they opened the door they heard Carole's voice. They looked at each other, and Aneesa gave her father a shove towards the kitchen. He sprinted across the living room carpet, hurdled the couch, flew into the kitchen and grabbed the phone.

"Carole? Carole? Don't hang up!"

"Ha-med, is that you? You sound a bit winded."

"Just walked through the door." Ha-med sat on the chair out of breath. Aneesa sat on his lap.

"So Ha-med, have you and Aneesa eaten?"

Carole invited them over for dinner at eight. She flew down the stairs, made a quick salad, climbed back up the steps two at a time, jumped in the shower and planned the main course.

The mirror stared at her with great admiration. Her time at the gym had returned obvious rewards: a body as firm as a girl's half her age. After two babies had taken their toll, a plastic surgeon had put her breasts back where they belonged, and tightened her post-partum belly as well. She slipped into black slacks and a rust-colored sweater that probed her torso as if it read brail.

She made angel hair pasta and three thick filets and a can of corn with diced peppers. She phoned the local deli.

"Saul, I need a favor. Can you get a strawberry cheesecake delivered to my home, now?"

"It shouldn't be a problem. I'll send one right over … if you tell me whom it's for." Saul had known Carole since he first opened thirty years before.

"That's none of your business … but between you and I … I think I'm in love."

Ha-med and Aneesa prepared for the evening. Aneesa insisted on wearing a white satin dress and a hair bow to match. They stopped at a florist on the way. Everyone knew Ms. Meyer, and the owner smiled as Ha-med asked what her favorite flowers were. He left with a magnificent fall bouquet. As they approached Carole's imposing neighborhood, Aneesa rolled down her window and stared in awe. With grand sprawling lawns and manicured gardens, palatial homes sat far back from the sidewalk-less street.

The entranceway gate to Ms. Meyer's estate opened as they approached and closed as they passed. As they parked behind Carole's Jag, Aneesa's eyes scanned the sculptures and gardens. When Aneesa reached up and pressed the fancy brass doorbell, symphonic chimes played *Claire de lune.*

"The door's open, just let yourselves in."

There stood a smiling Carole wearing an apron. She bent down and gave Aneesa a kiss as she handed Ms. Meyer the bouquet.

Next was a quick kiss on Ha-med's warm lips. Aneesa looked around and the tall winding banister caught her eyes.

"Aneesa, when I was your age, I'd sneak over when no one was watching, and slide down that very banister. Boy, would my father scream."

"What would he say, Carole?" said Aneesa, in a concerned, serious tone.

"Young lady, get down from there now! Will you not be satisfied until you break your neck?"

"Did you get in lots of trouble?" asked Annesa.

"Well, kinda. But guess what? I sure proved my father was wrong, because when I did fall off, I didn't break my neck ... I just fractured my arm!"

A soothing mist of warmth filled the air as Carole took Aneesa and guided her down the banister, and then said, "Well, shall we dine?"

As she escorted her guests through the foyer and into the dining room, Aneesa said: "Wow, this is bigger than my school cafeteria, but I bet the food is better here."

The bread and salad were already on the table, and the main course sat covered in the butler's pantry. Ha-med sat at the head, with his two favorite girls to either side. They held hands, closed their eyes, and Carole said; "Blessed our God, King of the Universe who brings forth bread from the earth."

After they ate, Aneesa insisted on cleaning up, so she and Carole gathered the dishes, made a pot of decaf, presented the cheesecake and the three retired to the living room. Aneesa asked if Carole would show them around so they went back and started the grand tour in the foyer. Carole directed their attention to the leaded glass dome illuminated overhead.

"It weighs over a thousand pounds, and is even more beautiful in the light of day."

An archway concealed massive wood pocket doors, which lead to the library two stories high. The corner housed a hundred year old Steinway grand. Aneesa sat down and played a quick minuet. The tour continued for half an hour, and then they headed back to the grand entranceway. She pointed at the beautiful, hand-carved paneled walls, then pushed on a section. A hidden doorway unveiled a steep stairway, which led to Carole's office. They walked down to find file cabinets, computer screens, keyboards, fax machines, several small televisions, and twenty-four hour financial news scrolling across a dedicated monitor.

"This used to be Grandpa Charlie's study. When he was a child, he was sent to America to live with his pharmacist uncle who raised him, and put him through medical school. He became a superb physician with a pharmacy background. He donated the land and money to build the clinic."

Carole lifted up Aneesa, hugged her, and continued: "The clinic that your father will soon be renovating."

She glanced at Ha-med, "Make Grandpa Charlie proud!"

She directed them to a soft reclining couch that faced a wall with diplomas and photos. When she pushed a button on the wall, footrests popped up, a white screen descended, a projector dropped out of the ceiling, lights dimmed, speakers popped out, and in amazing color and surround sound, *Shrek* played on the screen. When Shrek stomped, the couch that they sat on reverberated to his footsteps.

"This is my favorite movie," said Carole, while tickling Aneesa.

"I've watched it a thousand times!"

Aneesa agreed. Ha-med knew it was time to head home. It was a school night and Aneesa was struggling to keep her eyes opened.

"Would you two join me for Thanksgiving?" said Carole to smiles and nodding heads.

"I've not had a good Thanksgiving dinner in years," she said, kneeling down in front of Aneesa.

"Aneesa, would you please ask your grandparents to join us as well? My sons will be in. You can ask them your question."

"What question is that?" asked Ha-med

"It's girls stuff, Daddy."

Aneesa gave Carole the biggest hug she'd had in years. When they got to the front door, Aneesa lagged behind, not wanting to leave. Carole smiled at Ha-med while leaning against the door, blocking his exit. He leaned against her for a quick goodnight kiss.

His hands caressed the small of her back and he pressed his body firmly against hers. Her back arched and they kissed with enough passion that their pounding hearts shook the walls.

Their romantic prelude was interrupted by giggles from below. Aneesa was watching and laughing, and knew that they had forgotten she was there. The three of them huddled and hugged, never wanting to part.

On the way out the door Ha-med said, "It would please me to see you on Saturday night, though I would understand if you've made other plans."

"If I had made other plans, I would cancel them. See you Saturday."

"Is four o'clock a convenient time for you?"

She smiled, placed her hands together behind her back, leaned forward and gave him a quick peck on the cheek and said:"Perfect."

The following morning Ha-med and his bosses tweaked the plans while preparing for Monday's groundbreaking ceremony. The Board of Director's in construction attire will be providing the media a great photo-op.

Michael, Phyllis, and Kris stood more attentive then boot camp recruits under the direction of Drill Sergeant Hassan. They rolled out the blueprints and reviewed every fine detail and reviewed them again till they knew them by heart. Stoltz was just there to watch and observe, since on Monday at 10 he'd be heading to Europe.

Friday at 4:30 Ha-med said to his team, "Have a relaxing weekend – for the last time this year."

To the hush of silence he added: "C'mon guys, I was just kidding. Have a fun weekend. This is an exciting project. You should all be proud. See you on Monday."

On Ha-med's way home he went to the mosque to take part in the Jumma prayer and, as always the Imam was delighted to see him. Ha-med looked around and did not see the Sheik.

"Good evening Imam. So, where is our Sheik?"

"He's off visiting other mosques along the east coast. Boston, Chicago, Atlanta ... He will spend several days at a university in South Florida before he heads back to New York."

The elders were gathered around Afridi, laughing out loud at his stories. When Ha-med approached, Afridi's face filled with joy amidst welcoming hugs.

"Your face is a most welcomed sight," he said. "I'll never forget when I received a phone call from Mr. Ibrahim requesting my advice on what to do about yours and Sabira's raging hormones, as if I were an expert. For me, oral sex means telling dirty stories."

The two laughed, reminisced, and then joined their brothers for six o'clock prayers. When the prayer service ended Ha-med and Afridi quietly strolled away from the crowd. The old man detected Ha-med's sense of stress.

"Tell me Ha-med what troubles your mind?"

"Is a good Muslim Man permitted to fall in love with a Jewess?"

"It is more than a question of 'are we allowed to?' You will search till you locate the answer you seek. Muslim scholars permit Muslim men to marry nice Jewish girls. According to the wise Imam al-Tabar, al-Maa'idah verse 5:4 tells us yes, we are permitted to marry those women who first received the Scriptures from God."

"I find myself torn. I've recently met a woman. I've known her such a short time, but I feel our meeting was Allah's doing. Our lives and that of my daughter would be blessed if we join together as one."

"Is she a strong woman, whose heart will not break when her own people turn away? Are you, Ha-med, willing to accept similar reactions? Will you stand by her side and will she stand by yours if it turns out that these sides are the only you have? I have no answers, only questions. You must provide the answers. If you decide that she is the one, I would be honored to dance at your wedding."

He reminded Ha-med so much of Bassan. He bowed his head in thanks and respect, and the Imam welcomed them back to the Mosque.

"It is delightful to see the two of you immersed in such intense discussion. Is everything all right, Ha-med?" said the Imam.

The sincere concern from the Imam was comforting and gave Ha-med a renewed sense of belonging. "Yes Imam, everything's fine. Your concern for my well-being is a comfort in itself."

"Well, my office and ears are always opened to you. If you need to just talk, I'd be pleased to just listen. We have all missed you around here."

"Now that Aneesa is growing up and spends more time with her grandmother, my evenings are more flexible. I will try to come around more often."

Carole spent her morning with the Hospital Board, discussing Monday's groundbreaking ceremony. Then she attended a luncheon to help raise money for Breast Cancer Awareness. She pledged to provide funding for mammograms for all those in need. During lunch she ran into an old friend named Sheryl. They'd been the closest of friends since their youth but after Sheryl's divorce she and Carole had lost touch.

"Carole, you look wonderful," said Sheryl. "I thought of you so much when Ben died, but we had become so distant after my divorce, I didn't know what to do. I cried at the funeral for the loss of two dear friends, Ben and you."

"I really appreciated the card, and the contribution in Ben's name to plant trees in Israel was thoughtful … it's just what he would have wanted."

"If you have no plans this evening, would you care to join me at Temple?" said Sheryl.

"When did you start going to Shabbat Services?"

"I joined this Hebrew adult education class. I initially hoped to meet some single guys. Instead, I was re-acquainted with God. So, what do you say?"

Carole had not been to a service in years.

She smiled at Sheryl.

"I think I would like that. It may be just what I need. What time?"

"Eight o'clock sharp. The Rabbi gives dirty looks if you walk in a second late."

"Why don't we first meet for dinner over at Saul's at a quarter past six?" said Carole.

"Like the old days? Eh? Boy, we sure had some good times at Saul's."

They met over at Saul's and perused the menu and discussed old and new times over Matzo Ball soup. Sheryl again spoke of how grief-stricken she was when Dr. Meyer died.

"I cried at the funeral like we'd never lost touch. The crowd was enormous. Couldn't even get close. I wanted to call, but, y'know, felt kinda awkward. How long had it been?"

"I'd been meaning to call, but you know how it is, the time just flew by," said Carole.

As the conversation progressed and the wine took its toll, they each confessed the parts they had lifted, augmented, suctioned and tucked. Saul was greeting the guests, and was jolted when he noticed Carole and Sheryl sitting together. He walked over to their booth.

"What a sight for my sore old eyes. It's a *mecheieh* (a great pleasure)! I remember the two of you sitting right here when you were naïve little teens. It seems like yesterday. Where have the years gone?"

Saul winked at Carole. "So tell me my little Carole-a, how did *he* enjoy my cheesecake?"

"Tell me, Carole, you have a man?" said Sheryl with wide-opened eyes.

"Isn't it time for services by now? We'd better get going," said Carole, like a shy teen caught kissing a boy. As they left, they gave Saul big cozy hugs. When they went for their wallets, he pushed them away.

"This one's on the house, but I expect to see you two more often, no? Good Shabbas girls."

They left Sheryl's car at the deli, and got into Carole's.

At the instant the temple was in sight, Carole and her anxiety had a head-on collision. Her pulse raced and breaths shallowed. She pulled over, and stared at the building.

"Take some deep breaths, Carole. Are you OK?"

Her legs and her fingers were numb. After a few minutes, her breathing slowed down and the episode passed.

"Sorry 'bout that. That's not happened in years. After Ben died, my shrink said it was my brain's way of ignoring reality, or at least trying to."

"Are you sure you're alright? Would you like me to drive?"

"Actually, amazingly, I feel great. So many memories … births, deaths, Bar Mitzvahs, weddings, joys, sorrows … I guess I'd shut them out for too long. I feel terrific, let's go get me re-acquainted, shall we?"

They kissed the Mezuzah, grabbed prayer books, rushed in and sat down at a few minutes past eight. The Rabbi noticed them but in lieu of a stern rebuke, he gave Carole a smile. Following the traditional prayer service, he presented his sermon.

"The Torah provides us with so many lessons: to live by, to learn from, to share and pass on. My personal favorite is *Love thy neighbor.*

"Love Thy Neighbor? Three simple words, a simple philosophy, older than scripture itself. Everyone's heard it, everyone's said it, but who actually lives it?

According to Leviticus 19:18 … *thou shalt love thy neighbor as thou lovest thyself.* Well, at least we subscribe to the *lovest thyself* portion of the advice. The Hindus quote Mahabharata who said: … *do naught unto others that which would cause you pain.* Among Imam Al-Nawawi's Forty Hadiths it is written that *None of you truly believes until he wishes for his brothers what he wishes for himself.* A more contemporary version, with a slight variation was spoken by Socrates when he said ... *do not do to others that which would anger you if others did it to you.*

We live in tumultuous times. Extremists from the West Bank to Waco and from Korea to Kashmir seek an Inquisition. Who are these people? How dare they think they can hide behind false shields of religion! How can we love them when they do not love themselves?

They preach warfare, not welfare as they seek a monopoly on God.

During the Renaissance, Muslims, Christians and Jews forged symbiotic relationships. No sibling rivalry. No sabotaged plans. The outcome? Great advances for all of mankind. The Almighty looked down at his children, living as neighbors, loving as neighbors. He was proud.

Today, we again find ourselves living in a Renaissance – a technology Renaissance. The world is shrinking. We have unleashed the ability to communicate through boundaries and across borders. Physical obstacles and distance no longer impede our progress. People are living longer and closer.

But are we living better? Are we living freer? Freedom is the right to think and to share our thoughts without fear or obstruction. Fundamentalist extremists want to imprison our thoughts and enslave these freedoms.

Technology is the ultimate double-edged sword. Today, with the simple push of a button we can control a cancer, or move a mountain. We can also nullify a nation or eradicate the earth. Only we, together, living as neighbors can control which button is pressed next. Let us model our relationships after the Renaissance, not the Inquisition. Love thy Neighbor. Let us make the Almighty proud once again. *Cain Y'he Ratzon* – let it be God's will."

After the service there was a small reception to celebrate the Sabbath. The Rabbi blessed the food, and walked up to Carole.

"Why Ms. Carole Meyer, it's so nice to see you. And to what do we owe this guest appearance?"

Rabbi Steinberg knew Carole since her childhood, and Carole always enjoyed his wit and wisdom. He'd not seen her since Ben's funeral. They chatted of good times and bad. Carole felt welcomed, loved – part of a whole. The Rabbi smiled and asked her to stop by his office one afternoon. As she was leaving, the Rabbi gave her a hug and a smile.

"See you around?"

"That you can bet on," said Carole.

16

A Night on the Town

On Saturday morning Ha-med and Aneesa arrived at the Ibrahims' for piano lessons.

Aneesa ran ahead of her father, and as the Ibrahims opened the door, she said, "Grandma, do you think I could stay here tonight? Daddy and Carole have a date."

Ha-med did a quick double-take, shrugged his shoulders and went inside. Mrs. Ibrahim smiled. Mr. Ibrahim didn't. Ha-med stared at Aneesa, and admired her innocence. She looked baffled.

"Whaaat?"

The doorbell rang and Mrs. Berger came in.

"Don't worry, Grandpa," said Aneesa. "Carole is really nice. I know you will just love her."

With scales and arpeggios skipping along the keyboard, Mr. Ibrahim marched Ha-med and Babi into the kitchen. Momar's wary expression accompanied his paranoia. "Babi, this *Carole*, have you met her in secret?"

"No, I have not met her! I keep no secrets from you."

"How is it that you and my Granddaughter know of her, yet I have not before heard mention of her?"

"Aneesa was here late one evening, and as if often the case, you were out! She spoke of this Carole as her friend. You miss many of the comments she makes. The time will pass, and her youth will be gone. You will regret not watching her grow up."

Neither Momar or Ha-med could manage to squeeze in a word edge-wise. "And Momar, I do not pry, or accuse, but while we are on the topic, when you are out late, what are *you* doing? Who are you with?"

"I am at the mosque, in conversation or prayer. It is my inspiration. Besides, you are usually asleep by nine."

Tears pooled in Babi's swollen eyes.

"There was a time when I was your inspiration," she said.

Momar's defensive façade softened. "Babi, I know how hard you work at Mahshi's, and I understand that you are tired when you get home. But what am I to do with my time?"

He took her hands and looked into her eyes. "With Allah as my witness, you are still my inspiration."

The short stretch of silence seemed infinite.

Mrs. Ibrahim let out a rippling sigh, wiped her eyes, and spoke.

"Perhaps I can take afternoon naps when it is quiet at Mahshi's, and be there for you in the evening?" She paused, smiled, and then continued, "Promise me this – if I do stay awake, we will go out sometimes? Like we used to?"

Ha-med was relieved. The Ibrahims seemed to forget about Carole as they held hands, shared smiles and fell back in love. Ha-med quietly backed away from the table and tiptoed out the kitchen door. The crashing screen door shattered the air of solemnity. He froze in his tracks to the resound of his name.

"Muhammed Hassan. And where do you think you are going young man?" said Mr. Ibrahim. Ha-med turned and sighed, came back inside, smiled and sat down.

"Now Muhammed, tell Mrs. Ibrahim and I all about this *friend* of yours."

Ha-med spoke of Carole, her husband's accident, the picnic with Aneesa, the dinner at her house, and their sincere sense of compassion and love.

"It's like she woke up a part of me that I thought was long gone," said Ha-med. "And she lit a spark in Aneesa which I'd never seen."

Mr. Ibrahim placed his hand on Muhammed's shoulder.

"When my daughter passed on, the door to my heart slammed shut."

Mr. Ibrahim paused, took a deep breath, and continued, "Aneesa's warm glow tried to pry it opened, only to find the key jammed in the lock."

Mrs. Berger came in with Aneesa, and spoke proudly of her student and how much she reminded her of Sabira. As she left, Aneesa looked around at the somber faces and wet crumpled tissues.

"C'mon guys, it can't be that bad ... I'm hungry. Let's go to Mahshi's!" said Aneesa.

"First thing's first," said Momar. "Give your Grandpa a hug."

When they got to Mahshi's, the place was packed. The manager was a young man named Ishmael, who everyone called "Ishi".

His wife Fatima was the head waitress. The Ibrahims, Ha-med and Aneesa strolled in past the line and walked up to Ishmael.

"Hey Ishi, got a table?" said Mr. Ibrahim.

Ishi gazed over Aneesa's head at Mr. Ibrahim, pretending to not see her.

"I'm terribly sorry sir, but as you can see, we are really quite busy. If you do not have a reservation, it will be at least an hour before we can seat you."

He then looked down at Aneesa, smiled, and with a look of surprise, kissed her one cheek at a time.

"Oh, Ms. Aneesa, It is so nice to see you. Are these people here with you, my dear?"

"Yes sir, I brought them along. I'd like my usual table."

"Please follow me this way. Sorry for the delay. Your table is waiting. Fatima will be right with you."

Aneesa gave Ishi a wink and a smile, and Fatima escorted them to a table. During the meal, Grandma tried to distract Aneesa to allow the men to discuss Carole. Aneesa struggled to hear every word.

"Grandma, Shhhhh. Please, we're talking about Carole."

When dessert was delivered, Grandpa had an idea.

"Hey Aneesa, I'm pretty full, couldn't eat another thing. No room for this cake or ice cream. Will you walk over to the park with me?"

"Grandpa? You must just be kidding. This is my most favorite part of the whole meal!"

"And I must agree with Aneesa, " said Mrs. Ibrahim. "I would not miss this part even if I was full."

"Dad, if you really feel like going for a walk, I'd hate for you to go alone. I'll join you, but lets hurry back, OK?" said Ha-med.

So Ha-med and Mr. Ibrahim took a walk to the park and sat on a bench.

"So, my Ha-med, you have fallen in love with a Jewess. They are the *people of the book.* But remember, whether Jew, or Muslim, you are forbidden to know this woman unless you are husband and wife!"

Momar and Ha-med gazed into each other's eyes and for the first time in years they were father and son.

"Your burden may be heavier than you can perceive through the dense fog of love."

Momar placed his hands on Ha-med's shoulders and continued.

You must be a man, for your sake, for her sake, and the sake of your daughter. You must marry, or bid her farewell. There can be no other way. If you two are wed, they will call her your wife. If you are not, they will call her your Jewish whore."

The clouds of the overcast sky were soothing. There were birds in the trees being chased by the squirrels; a young couple was kissing; bicycles cruising, dogs being walked and kites up above. Men playing dominos, woman with cards and some boys about ten playing ball in a field. A baseball rolled right up to Momar's feet and came to a halt. He picked it up and saw a handsome young boy with curly brown hair and an olive complexion. He wore jeans and a sweatshirt with an American flag, and a baseball cap turned with the front to the back. He looked as though he'd stepped right out of a *Gap Kids* commercial.

Momar stood up, wound up, and threw him the ball. The boy caught it, smiled, and walked up to the bench.

"Thank you so much sir, would you like to play?"

Trailing behind and watching their son was his African-American father, and attractive white mom with one in a stroller, and one on the way. Mr. Ibrahim winked at the father and spoke to the boy.

"What is your name, young man?"

"Tyler. Tyler Jackson, Sir."

"Well, Master Tyler Jackson, thank you so much for the invitation. Perhaps some other time? Our family is expecting us at any moment. Can I get a rain check?"

"Yes sir. We play every Saturday." He turned to Ha-med. "And you can come too."

Ha-med and Momar strolled back to Mahshi's with a fresh outlook on life. After dessert, they drove back to the Ibrahims'.

"Go out, and have a pleasant evening, but heed my advice."

He paused, smiled, and continued, "And next Saturday night you are watching Aneesa. Mrs. Ibrahim and I are going out."

Ms. Meyer woke up at a quarter past ten. She went to the gym, unheard of for her on a normal Saturday morning.

"So what's the occasion?" said the man at the desk. Carole smiled, strutted by and went straight to the treadmill. After three miles, she hit the weights. After her shower she was off to the spa for her hair and her nails.

Her flamboyant hairdresser, J. Michael, looked up at her.

"Hi sweetie. I've not seen you here on a Saturday in years!" He gave her a hug, and a kiss on each cheek. "So tell me, who's the lucky guy?"

She told him a little, while keeping him guessing, but told him that this was her first date in years.

When she got home, she tried on a dozen outfits and then phoned J. Michael. "OK, ya got me," said Carole. "He's tall, dark, dreamy, and I think he's the one … so … what do I wear?"

"A simple black dress. Pearls. No bra. A sexy mink. Light on the make-up, and a wisp of *Joy de Jean Patou*."

At five minutes to four Ha-med pulled into her driveway. His car had just been detailed, as had his beard.

She stared out the window as Ha-med approached in a black cashmere jacket, fine wool gray slacks, a brand new white shirt and a burgundy tie.

He was carrying a dozen red roses.

She opened the door. Cut at mid-thigh, her simple black dress had an open back, and exquisite pearls peaked through her sultry black mink.

He placed his lips gently on hers as they strolled to the kitchen. In the kitchen she admired the roses but more so, Ha-med. As she turned and stretched to reach for a vase, her dress hiked up and revealed her thighs. He reached from behind her and grabbed the vase from the shelf. She leaned back against him. His lips and her neck fit like parts of a puzzle. His pulsating body pressed against hers and she turned and looked up into his eyes. Ha-med tensed-up and froze as he recalled Mr. Ibrahim's words.

"Is everything all right? Did I do something wrong?" said Carole.

"Carole Meyer, I love you so much, it hurts," He hugged her endearingly, and continued, "Let's just go out and have a great time. Later, I'll speak from my heart."

The tension dissolved as they drove through the tunnel. Carole was reassured by the warmth of his hand and gave him a kiss on the cheek. When they exited the tunnel, his eyes were as blinding as scrolling marquees and his smile as bright as the dazzling signs. He never grew tired of New York's bright lights; Carole never grew tired of his little-boy look. The dinner and show were delightful, and afterwards Carole and Ha-med strolled, cuddled tight through the brisk evening air.

They went to a piano bar on the top floor of a building and sat in a corner booth lit by a single votive.

The East River shimmered and an entertainer named Robert played piano and sang.

A crescent-moon glowed.

Bob played piano and crooned love songs while Ha-med and Carole held hands and shared hearts.

"So tell me my Ha-med, please don't break your promise." She placed her hands in his and continued, "Speak from your heart ... what's on your mind?"

Ha-med gazed into her eyes. His obvious nervousness made Carole anxious. She released his hands and started to arrange the perfectly organized tabletop. He cleared his throat, swallowed and spoke.

"We have known each other for such a short time, yet I feel I have known you for years and I need to be sure that you have the same feelings towards me that I have for you, and I don't-- "

Carole interrupted her trembling man by placing her finger on his lips in mid-sentence. She rubbed and kissed his hands to warm them up.

"Muhammed Hassan, if it was proper, I would kneel before you and ask for your hand."

She leaned toward him and whispered, "Does that answer your question?"

While still holding hands, he took a deep breath and knelt down to the sounds of their two pounding hearts. He gathered his thoughts and looked into her eyes.

"Carole Meyer, will you be my wife?"

The flickering candle highlighted the tears running down her cheeks. An audience witnessed their stellar performance as onlookers watched him rise up from the floor. Bob played and sang matrimonial tunes as the waiter poured champagne.

"It's on the house," he said.

They left a generous tip and strolled out engaged.

"Carole, let's get married on Thanksgiving weekend. Your sons will be home. I'll speak with the Imam, you speak with the Rabbi, perhaps we can all meet for dinner this week?"

When they got in the car, Ha-med said: "Would you like to join me in telling Aneesa the news?"

They drove to the Ibrahim's and tiptoed into Aneesa's room. Mrs. Ibrahim woke when she heard the door open. She put on a robe and turned on some lights.

"So this must be your Carole," she said to Ha-med. She turned to Carole and continued, "Aneesa told me all about you. It is a pleasure to finally meet you."

They hugged each other like family. Aneesa was smiling, half awake. The next one to awaken was Momar.

"It's one o'clock in the morning! What's all the noise?"

He then noticed Carole, smiled, and everyone noticed his outfit. No shoes, no shirt, loose boxer shorts and a red face. He looked up to the heavens, shrugged his bare shoulders, smiled at his wife and went back to bed.

As all mothers do when they want to keep talking, Babi said, "Let's go to the kitchen, I'll make us a snack."

Carole followed her. Ha-med sat alone with Aneesa, hugged her, and looked into her eyes.

"If I ask you a secret question, do you promise to keep it between just you and me, for a little while at least?"

She sat up, and looked right into her father's eyes, "OK Daddy, I'm ready."

"May I have your permission to marry Ms. Carole?" said Ha-med.

Aneesa's eyes popped open. She jumped up, spun out of the room laughing and flew into Carole's arms.

"Can I start calling you Mommy right now? Can I call my new brothers?"

A few paces behind, Ha-med found a joyous kitchen with three women hugging, laughing, and crying all at the same time. Momar again appeared, this time in pajamas, slippers, and a bathrobe that he never wore.

"Now what's all the noise?"

In a slow sing-songy voice Aneesa said, "Grandpa?" She paused, took a deep breath, then continued, "Carole and my father are getting married."

The five sat down and made plans.

"Carole and I would like to be married on the Saturday after Thanksgiving," said Ha-med.

"Please join us at my home for Thanksgiving dinner, and to meet my sons."

"So what kind of a wedding do you plan to have?" said Mrs. Ibrahim. "And where will it be?"

"We'd first like to meet together with our Imam, and Carole's Rabbi. Perhaps we can arrange a dinner at Mahshi's?"

Momar and Babi held hands and smiled.

"We will have the wedding party at Mahshi's, and I will pay for it," said Momar as he stood up from the table, scanned the happy faces, and continued, "And now I am finally going to bed!"

When he reached his bedroom door, he said, "And remember, you are not married yet!"

Aneesa jumped up, put a hand on each of Carole's cheeks, and in a serious tone said: "Good heavens. What ever am I going to wear?"

17

Groundbreaking

A cool blinding sun lit the Old Cohen Clinic as Ha-med and McDaniel stepped out of their truck. They handed out hard hats and gold-plated shovels to members of the board. Flanked by cameras and crews beneath crispy blue skies, everyone smiled and posed for the cameras.

A man from the news yelled, "Which one of you is the chairman of the board?"

To his surprise, the *chairman* tipped her hardhat revealing long silky hair and a soft glowing smile.

Shovel in hand, Carole said, "That would be me."

"So, how does it feel to finally break ground after so many months of planning?"

"Months? It's been a lifetime. It's a wonderful feeling. I've dreamt of this moment ever since I can remember."

She proceeded to pay homage to Dr. Charles Cohen. Most did not know that she was not only his granddaughter, but his sole heir as well.

"My Grandfather must be so honored as he looks down upon us from heaven above."

Another reporter yelled. "How'd you choose this team for the renovation?"

"That was the easy part. No others even came close. Mr. Hassan and his group not only understood the physical design concept, but grasped the emotional nature of the project as well."

She directed everyone's attention towards Ha-med.

"Mr. Hassan, why don't you tell them about the project."

The cameras and mics followed Mr. Hassan as he walked and stood close beside Carole.

"This moment is a fantasy realized, a dream come true. A long time ago in a land far away a wise old man said to me: *May God grant you the ability to contribute good things to the world, and the capacity to find joy in the things that you do.* This project is the epitome of his words."

His charm and charisma won over the crowd. The cameras loved him.

Mr. Kahane approached in a wheelchair. He noticed how Carole's dreamy eyes followed Mr. Hassan's every move. He loved her like a daughter, had danced at her wedding and watched her suffer when Benjamin died.

When Ha-med finished speaking, a reporter from *The Post* motioned to Ha-med.

"Can we get a picture of just the two of you?"

As Carole moved closer to Ha-med, she noticed Kahane. She struggled to hold back her tears. She posed for the cameras and yelled to the crowd.

"Today's event comes one month before a long-standing Cohen Clinic tradition. Thanks to the generosity of those like Mr. Kahane, every Thanksgiving Sunday since this place was built, the less fortunate have been invited to join us for lunch. Mr. Hassan and I will be serving the food, so I invite you to join us and lend us a hand."

Ha-med was astonished when he walked toward the curb. Lining the street were media trucks and vans boasting bright logos and letters. The commotion was a public relations bonanza for Ha-med and his firm.

Among the flashy caravan of TV trucks was another that went unnoticed. An unmarked black utility van attracted little attention.

Seated within it was the Sheik from Palestine and his two bodyguards. They peered through the windows with telescopic lenses and recorded on tape the entire event. The console was right out of James Bond meets Bill Gates. A wireless Internet hook-up provided a hacker's paradise to data banks all over the world.

McDaniel, Ha-med and Ms. Meyer stood chatting. Carole excused herself, and walked over to Kahane. "Your grandfather and I were the closest of friends, he was more like a brother to me than a friend," said Kahane.

"I miss Grandfather, too. I sure would enjoy it you stopped by the house on Thanksgiving. I will have some people over, and my kids will be in from college." As his limo pulled up, he said he would try.

The cameras inside the sheik's van kept on rolling. The Sheik entered Kahane's photo on an international search. He fumed with anger as an impressive resume flashed up on the screen.

Moshe Kahane, aka Michael K. Haney, aka Mr. Hanes. His *Hanes' Bros. Jewelers* were found in the malls and in strip shopping centers all over the world. The diamonds he sold were from his personal diamond mines. Kahane kept his Lear Jet and yacht off the coast of Greece. He owned health spas, several theatres, shopping malls, car dealerships – even a pro football team. His wealth remained hidden from most of the world by funneling his profits through his non-profit charitable foundation. He had three names and addresses in three different countries, and supported the Jewish Defense League, World Jewish Congress, and several Zionist organizations.

The Sheik's evil mind began ticking away as a plan formulated within his sick head. "Cohen? Meyer? Kahane? And that Jew-loving Hassan? All together for a delightful Thanksgiving Sunday afternoon to feed the poor. How touching, like the last supper."

Sheik Khalil felt like he had just hit the lotto. Panning the camera, he zoomed in on a park bench just two blocks away.

"That's where I'll sit as they enjoy their last meal," said the Sheik. As he scanned the park through his lens, he noticed a photographer was admiring his van. They photographed him while he photographed them. They traced his steps. He got into the news van parked right behind theirs. The Sheik-driven van sped off to an abandoned Newark, New Jersey warehouse.

The festivities continued with snacks in the hospital lobby, while prying reporters searched hard for an angle. A particularly obnoxious one said to Carole: "So, how well do you know Muhammed Hassan?"

"Our relationship is strictly professional. His plans for the clinic are fantastic!" said Carole.

As the reporter was about to proceed with more questions, Ha-med stared him down, cut him off, and said:

"Thank you so much for this enthusiastic welcome. I promise my team will make everyone proud."

Ha-med shook Carole's hand in a business-like fashion then smiled and walked out to survey the grounds.

The following morning under Ha-med's direction, crews and equipment were ready by eight. Carole drove up and tapped on her horn. Ha-med approached her window as she rolled it down and showed off their picture on the front page of *The Times*.

The caption read: "Ms. Carole Meyer and Mr. Muhammed Hassan break ground for the long awaited Cohen Clinic Renovation." He leaned into her car and gave her a big kiss.

"Join me and Aneesa this evening for dinner?"

"I wouldn't miss it for the world. How's about seven?"

"Perfect, see ya then." She drove off with applause in the background from the audience of workers who witnessed the kiss.

That evening, Ha-med served a delightful dinner. After they finished, the three of them cleaned up and relaxed on the couch. In minutes Aneesa was out like a light upon Carole's warm lap. Ha-med put her to bed, then sat down beside Carole.

Their lips became locked and their bodies entwined. They merged on the couch with meandering minds, wandering hands, and sizzling thoughts. Tempted by passion they thought of Aneesa and slowly pulled back. These born-again virgins were put to the test.

"I'd better get going," said Carole.

"Carole, I love you so much," whispered Ha-med with a forceful embrace.

She stood up. With a frustrated – but sexy – smirk, she shook her head slowly.

"Good night my darling handsome Ha-med."

The next morning she drove up to the jobsite, again with a newspaper in hand, but this time it was *The Daily Inquisitor*. Its cover was a full-color photograph of a passionate kiss through Carole's car window.

The caption read: "Oops! Jewish Socialite and Arab Architect get caught in the Act."

Carole was livid. Ha-med looked at her and could not restrain his laughter. His smile overpowered her fuming expression and he leaned in and planted another big kiss on her lips. "I guess it's time to announce our engagement."

The week passed quickly, and on Friday evening Carole went to Temple and Ha-med to his mosque. Carole told the Rabbi about her fiancé.

Ha-med and the Imam spoke at length as well. The foursome made plans to meet at Mahshi's on Sunday for lunch.

A few moments before sunset, Ha-med was at the mosque enjoying conversation when The Sheik stalked in, his daunting imps alongside.

The Imam rushed over.

"Assalaam alaikum, how was your trip?"

"Wa alaikum Assalaam." The Sheik hugged the Imam.

"Welcome back. Did you have a good journey along the east coast?" said Mr. Ibrahim.

I had a most productive journey," said the Sheik, while attracting his usual crowd. "I met with large groups of young Muslim men. The universities welcomed me with open arms, and open wallets. Our brothers in South Florida have raised millions to further our mission."

"Excuse me for asking, but just what is your mission?" asked Ha-med.

"We spread the teachings of our Prophet, Muhammad. We teach our children to be proud of who they are and of what they are – Muslims! This country threatens our very existence. If the world will not respect us, we will teach it to fear us."

He paused and then looked right at Ha-med.

"Some amongst us have even stooped down to the level of rich Jewish whores."

"I beg your pardon, wise Sheik," said Ha-med, slowly and clearly, "*Whore* denotes a carnal relationship has occurred!"

Ha-med paused, and his tone became loud and dogmatic. "If this is not the case, then such accusations are slanderous lies. Allah punishes those whose tongues spread deceit!"

The Imam struck his fist on the table. "It's time for our prayers. This is Allah's house! Back off or leave!"

The Sheik was determined to get the last word in and lifted his crippled scarred hand. "This *woman* I speak of is still but a Jewess. Are *our* women not worthy enough for Jew-loving traitors?"

Afridi caught Ha-med's eyes, and gave him the "T" sign for time-out.

Ha-med acquiesced. The prayer service was plagued by unrest and distraction as whispers and rumors gained momentum.

"How dare Ha-med have the nerve to insult our wise guest."

"Ha-med prefers Dr. Dahij and his *love thy neighbor* bullshit?"

"What is this we hear? He prefers Jewish whores to fine Muslim women?"

When the prayer service ended the teens flocked to the Sheik as he reminded them that just a short time ago the mosque had been vandalized.

"Beware of those liars who call themselves Muslims, while trying to blend in with everyone else. Emit Dahij? Thinks he's a Messiah? Prefers Jews and Christians for friends. *Seize them and kill them wherever you find them ... do not befriend the Christian or Jew.* This is what our sacred Koran commands us."

"You are a visitor, a guest in America. This country has freedom. If you are so miserable here, go back home," said Ha-med.

"This Zionist Country wants our existence squashed. We will no longer stand by and tolerate this."

The Sheik gazed aimlessly into space as his heartbeats of hatred kept ticking away. Suddenly, he mellowed and spoke in an uncharacteristically calm tone.

"Jihad Time is upon us and we must unite." He then turned, walked out the door and disappeared into the night.

A dozen or so members of the Islamic Youth Group began shouting. Enraged and chanting, the mob stormed out onto the neighborhood streets.

"Jihad Time is upon us – We must unite."

"Jihad Time is upon us – Allah is Great."

Someone hurled a brick through the window of a small kosher diner, and another broke the glass at nearby Mel's Clothing Store. Spray-painted slogans of hatred followed suit.

When squad cars and paddy wagons arrived on the scene, the Sheik from Palestine was nowhere to be found. Ha-med caught the tail end of a flat-black utility van speeding away. He scratched his head. He could not place it. He knew he'd seen that van somewhere before.

When the mob disbanded, Ha-med, Mr. Ibrahim and Afridi sat with the Imam in his office. Two police officers arrived; this now-troubled mosque had some questions to answer.

"Who is this elusive Sheik who is inciting havoc and bigotry in your congregation?" said an officer, as the four witnesses volunteered information.

"He is an educated, well published popular sheik. He attracts new young members into our mosque. They find him exciting, intriguing," said the Imam.

"He is tall, over six feet, has a long flowing beard, and always wears black. He calls himself Sheik Ahmed Muhammed Khalil," said Afridi.

"His left hand is crippled, with only three fingers, and these are deformed," said Ha-med.

"I saw them drive off in a black van with a satellite dish," said Mr. Ibrahim.

Ha-med sprung up from the table like a Jack-in-the-Box.

"I saw that van just the other day a few miles from here. It was at the groundbreaking ceremony for the Cohen Clinic Renovation Project."

The Imam sighed, leaning back.

"When Khalil first arrived, his impressive credentials overpowered his extremist ideals. He has spoken all over the world, in mosques from London to Florida. The more time he spends here, the more we can see that he is trouble."

He cleared his throat and continued, "Now what do we do?"

"We would appreciate your cooperation down at the station. Our Detective Francisco has worked these cases before," said a police officer.

The Imam said they would be glad to assist, and they all agreed to go down the next day at noon.

Mrs. Ibrahim was at home pacing in fear. It was after midnight.

Aneesa had been sleeping for hours. Her husband and Ha-med were usually home by now and she saw reports on the news of trouble at the mosque. She heard cars in the driveway, turned on the lights and waited by the door.

Her frazzled husband and son-in-law got out of their cars as she opened the door. She brewed coffee as they nervously recounted what had happened. Aneesa had piano at ten in the morning so Ha-med spent the night on the couch. He telephoned Carole, filled her in on the evening's events, and asked if she would join him at the police station.

"Yes, my Ha-med. I will come by the Ibrahim's in the morning. Good night. I love you, forever."

18

Detective Francisco

Carole's new life was just coasting along until some extremist Sheik formed speed bumps in the road. So much to be thankful for as Thanksgiving approached; yet her anxiety level was at an all time high. Her over-crammed mind was about to explode. The usual influx of holiday pleas; her sons coming home to meet Ha-med; the Rabbi and Imam meeting for lunch; a wedding to plan; the Sunday free lunch.

She drove over to the Ibrahim's before Aneesa's piano lesson at ten and as she was about to ring the bell, her daughter-to-be flung open the door and jumped into her arms. She kissed her and smiled.

"Good morning, Mom."

Carole carried her into the kitchen and caught the Ibrahims in a tender embrace. Carole cleared her throat. Aneesa giggled.

"Grandma, we are having a wedding in just a few weeks!" said Aneesa in an excited, nervous tone. "I still don't know what I'm going to wear!"

"One day this week, how 'bout us three ladies go do some serious shopping?" said Carole.

Babi whipped up a quick meal; they planned a small cozy wedding, and proceeded to design the invitations to read:

It is with great pleasure that
MUHAMMED HASSAN& CAROLE MEYER
Request the honor of your presence as we say our vows
And join in holy matrimony
On Saturday, November the seventeenth at three o'clock in the afternoon
At the County Courthouse Annex
Reception immediately following at Mahshi's

Ha-med had just gotten out of the shower and wandered into the kitchen clad in wet hair and a towel. To his surprise, he found the wedding planners feverishly working out every detail.

The doorbell rang again, Ha-med ran to get dressed, and Aneesa welcomed Mrs. Berger inside. As she jumped up on the piano bench, she said: "Mrs. Berger, do you know how to play *Here Comes The Bride?*"

Mrs. Berger proceeded to play a fantastic medley of matrimonial melodies and then Aneesa sat down for her lesson.

Ha-med and Carole drove into town and their first stop was the print shop. They chose Ivory card stock and burgundy ink and waited until the invitations were printed and then sprinted over to the post office for stamps. As they casually strolled back to the car, Ha-med suddenly realized that Carole was gone. For a split second he was panic-stricken. She had ducked into a store and as he passed by, she snuck up behind him, covered his eyes and said, "Guess who?"

It that transient moment of concern, he realized how strong his love was for Carole. He lifted her up, placed her over his shoulder and carried her back to the car.

They drove back to the Ibrahim's and organized an assembly line on the dining room table. Carole addressed the envelopes, Mr. Ibrahim stuffed them with invitations, Aneesa licked them, Mrs. Ibrahim sealed them, then Ha-med stamped them and stacked them in a box. Ha-med, Carole, and Momar dropped them off at the post office on their way to the police station.

They strolled into the lobby and Ha-med introduced Carole to Afridi and the Imam and then a police escort guided them to a messy conference room with a fresh pot of coffee, stale Krispy Kremes, Styrofoam cups, small red plastic straws, no napkins, no plates, and a disorganized pile of mug shots.

They all took their seats and Detective Felix Francisco walked in. This weathered detective was stocky, not fat. He stood five feet eight inches tall with the stance of a prizefighter. His receding hairline helped augment his mustache that more than made up for what he lacked on his scalp. His nose was crooked from all of its' fractures. He was crude, painfully honest, and got right to the point in his thick New York accent. He circled the room and sized ever body up. "I really appreciate you guys comin' in. Let's get started." He directed his first question to the Imam.

"So, how long's this Sheik's been in town? Who invited him? Where's he from?"

"A few months ago I received a phone call from a man representing a respected mosque in New Jersey. They faxed some information about Khalil, and said he had a very busy schedule but would be willing to speak to our youth."

"So, what else can anyone tell me about this guy?"

"He drives around in a black van with two guards," said Ha-med.

"When he spoke at a mosque in London, it was the biggest crowd they ever had seen!" said the Imam.

"We heard that young Muslims poured in when he spoke, " said Afridi. "Although some of his writings were radically slanted, we struggle to get young ones into our mosque. The attendance at our Islamic Youth Group meetings has tripled since his arrival."

Detective Francisco yelled out the door to anyone who might be listening. "Fetch me a sketch artist. Now!" Within minutes a man appeared with pencil and pad. They went around the table describing the Sheik's features.

"He is over six feet tall, about six-three," said Afridi.

"His face is a long drawn-out oval, with a pointy chin beneath a long flowing beard," said Mr. Ibrahim.

"His bushy eyebrows just about cover his beady eyes," said Ha-med. He paused, looked at Carole, held her hand, and continued, "He has thick, weathered olive skin, and crevices on his forehead and cheeks."

"His nose has a hump and a long drooping tip, almost touching his thick upper lip!" said Afridi.

"His right hand always clutches a leather Koran," said the Imam, who took a deep breath, and continued, "And his left hand is crippled with only three fingers, and these are deformed. His thumb is almost normal, but has no finger nail and its tip is scarred."

The frightening sketch of the face and the hand made Carole bury her head on Ha-meds chest.

Francisco handed out his business cards.

"If you guys come up with anything else, call me immediately. Thanks again for comin' in."

"Do you think this man is dangerous?" asked Carole.

"Put it this way darlin', better safe than sorry. When I find him, I'll be sure to ask him."

They all walked out together and the Imam took Carole aside. "Carole, it is a pleasure to meet you although I wish it was under more pleasant circumstances. Rabbi Steinberg and I go way back. I look forward to seeing you tomorrow for lunch at Mahshi's. What's a good time?"

"How's about two?"

"I'll be there with an appetite. See you tomorrow."

19

Metamorphosis

A neglected warehouse by the Newark docks was not as abandoned as its neighbors perceived. A black van drove up to its heavy steel door. The Sheik grabbed some controls and pushed a button as his reverberating voice bellowed, "Open Sesame."

A rickety metal door, badly rusted, screeched up and out of the way to expose welcoming bows from a half-dozen turbaned and bearded auto mechanics.

Out-of-place at a desk sat a young man with a crew-cut. Billy Kowalski was an enterprising manipulative custom car magician. He was raised on the street stealing cars for a living. When he got out of prison, his talent and luck landed him a job at the U.S. Government's automotive weapons division.

The Sheik marched over to Billy, "Here is a down payment,"he said as he dropped a thick crisp wad of fresh hundred dollar bills on the desk.

Billy flipped through the stack, and said, "Where's the rest?"

"First let us see if your abilities merit your fee. Don't disappoint me!" Billy nodded and smiled. He was smart enough not to argue with Khalil. The Sheik and his guards took the elevator upstairs.

The van was hauled up on a lift and the team converged upon it armed with welding equipment, high-power tools, a paint module and a well thought out plan. A metamorphosis was underway.

The vehicle was primed, and then several coats of fire-truck red paint were professionally applied and baked on. Bright lights were mounted on its roof, an emergency license plate was screwed on, ambulance signs with white crosses were placed in position, and its' solid steel frame was adjusted and welded.

To loud shrieks of "Jihad," bulletproof glass was put to the test, as a man with an Uzi fired away. Billy did not find this display the least bit amusing.

Billy ate his lunch while the rest rolled out their mats, bowed down and faced Mecca. Then they got back to work. The van's interior was stripped roof to floor, wall-to-wall, front to back. All that remained was a solid empty shell with a console and driver's seat. Under Billy's direction, two munitions experts arrived, backed their van up to the warehouse, and with a forklift unloaded an enormous wooden crate. They got to work. When they finished, the gutted, bulletproof steel truck was a two thousand-pound bomb disguised as an ambulance.

Upstairs at a desk the Sheik drew out plans to deliver this gift to the Charles Cohen Clinic. With guards at his sides he sketched, reviewed maps and made detailed notes.

He tore off the page and put it in his pocket. He took a deep breath, and firmly inscribed *Emit Dahij* onto the pad. He stared at the name with inconceivable intensity.

The Sheik grabbed the pencil, slammed it down on the table and it snapped in two. The palm of his crippled hand came crashing down next to the broken pieces. He scribbled some words, gazed with disgust, tore the sheet off the pad, crumpled the page and lit a match to it.

Next, he collapsed on the couch, falling quickly asleep under the careful watch of his petrified guards.

As moonlight accompanied the ship's blinding beacons, foghorns awakened Sheik Khalil. He and his guards rode the elevator back down to the workshop. As the door opened, they were in awe. A magnificent "ambulance" greeted them. He congratulated his team, praised Allah, and handed another wad of bills to Mr. Kowalski. The room filled with shadows of Arabic whispers. Evil expressions loomed behind Billy's back.

The Imam, The Rabbi, Carole, Ha-med, the Ibrahims and Aneesa converged on Mahshi's for lunch. The Imam and Rabbi hugged with words of "*Assalaam alaikum*" and "*Aleichem Shalom.*" Carole stood up and introduced the Rabbi. Aneesa stood at Carole's side.

"Hey, I have a great idea!" said Aneesa. She eyeballed all in attendance, and continued, "Since we are all here anyway, why don't my father and Carole just get married now?"

Everyone smiled and no one disagreed. The mood was set for a most pleasant lunch. Ishi escorted them to a table, and Fatima served them a feast with the Rabbi's dietary restrictions in mind.

Ha-med broke the ice.

"Carole and I have both been married before; me in a mosque, Carole in a temple. This time we plan to say our vows in the courthouse. We ask that you please join us and give us your blessings."

The Imam suggested that Carole convert. The Rabbi suggested Ha-med do the same. They knew these suggestions were futile. They enjoyed their meal – the wedding was set for Saturday at three at the courthouse.

After the Imam and Rabbi left, the rest of the festivities were finalized with several busy days ahead.

On Thanksgiving Thursday a dinner would be served at Carole's. On Friday Ha-med would go pray at the mosque while Carole and Sheryl would spend the evening at Temple. On Saturday at two, they'd meet at the courthouse followed by a celebration at Mahshi's. On Sunday the Clinic Thanksgiving Feast would take place.

For Ha-med and Carole, the next few weeks crawled by, but for everyone else they flashed. The Ibrahims planned an Arabic feast. Saul planned a white wedding cake and a chocolate groom's cake. Ha-med booked the romantic, ocean-view suite at a five-star resort in the Hamptons. At the wedding, they planned to politely greet the guests, but did not intend to stick around all night.

Disheveled and stressed, Detective Francisco rifled through files and photos but no new leads were forthcoming. He had more intuition than a group of old ladies and these sorts of cases filled him with trepidation.

"The Sheik disappears and reappears, but where does he go? Who is he with? What is he up to?"

Francisco paced, looked at more photos, looked at the sketch and reviewed his notes. The desk sergeant came in with a fresh pot of coffee and a box of donuts.

"Anything you need?"

"Yeah. Tell me where the Sheik is, and what he's up to … and, oh yeah, find his van."

Francisco's own words echoed inside his head, " … his Van!"

It had been seen parked outside the clinic during the ceremony. The place had been swarming with cameras; surely someone must have caught it on tape!

The sergeant was about to speak as Francisco grabbed his old brown leather flight jacket and flew out the door. He sped over to the Cohen Clinic. When he found Ha-med, he honked his horn and shouted out the window.

"Hey, Ha-med, let's take a ride."

Ha-med tried to climb into the Detective's beat up Ford truck but found the door was jammed.

"You gotta get in on my side," said the detective.

Francisco stepped out, Ha-med pushed away stale donuts and slid across the coffee-stained seat. He tried to open the window. No such luck. It was also stuck.

"So what's this about? Where are we going?"

Attempting a W.C. Fields impersonation, the detective said, "Patience my son, patience."

They drove to a local TV station.

Francisco strutted in like he owned the place and a cute skinny blonde put down her nail file and greeted him sarcastically.

"Detective Francisco, what a pleasant surprise," she said, popping her chewing gum. "So tell me, Detective, what is it this time?"

"Honey, you act like the only time I come around is when I need your help."

"Cut the crap, *Honey*, jus' get to the point."

He asked her about video footage from the Clinic groundbreaking.

"I think Bobby was tapin' that day, if you sit back a minute I'll give him a call." She dialed his phone, filed her nails and turned on the speakerphone.

"Channel Four News, Bobby here."

"Hey Bobby, guess who's wantin' a favor?"

"Hey detective, whatsup?"

"Hey Bobby, how are things goin' ... how's that ticket I made disappear last month?"

Minutes later Bobby located the footage and sat down at a console with Ha-med. Francisco stood behind Ha-med like the coach in the corner of the ring.

"Here's where I need your help," said Francisco. "Somewhere in these tapes there must be a shot of a black van out front of the clinic. Keep your eyes peeled. Find it! OK Bobby, let's roll."

For over an hour, Ha-med's eyes were fixed on the monitor. Several false alarms gave Francisco false hope. Ha-med began yawning, but his eyes remained glued to the screen. Francisco paced; Bobby leaned back and snored; Ha-med didn't flinch.

"Quick! Stop! Roll back the tape!" yelled Ha-med, startling the others. Bobby fell off his rolling chair, got up off the floor and hit the pause button. The three of them stood watching frame by frame in reverse.

There it was. The street with the TV vans was seen off in the distance. Bobby zoomed in, tightened the focus, and the Sheik's van was seen wedged between two news trucks. It was a late-model Chevy, but the license plate was blocked. They focused on the van parked right behind it. It said KAVU. Francisco thanked Bobby with a handshake and the blonde with a pat on the rear.

"Francisco, you owe me!" she said.

The detective dropped off Ha-med back at the clinic and then drove over to the KAVU studios. He walked up to the counter and was greeted by an articulate blonde man in his thirties with a fresh haircut, a suit, and a goofy smile plastered on his clean-shaven face.

"Good day to you, kind sir. And how may *we* help you?"

Francisco was in no mood for actors. "*We*? Who the hell are *we*? *You* can help *me* by shutting the hell up, and getting your boss!"

"Well, excuse me for living, but who may I say is calling?"

"Just tell him Francisco." He whipped out his badge and a glimpse of his gun.

"I guess if I don't hurry, the next thing you'll say is *Go 'head, Make My Day.*" The man in the suit waltzed into the newsroom.

"Some rude detective has a serious attitude problem. Thinks he's something special. His name is Francisco."

The station director, C. Stewart Winchell, walked out and gave Francisco a brotherly bear hug.

"Felix! It's been too long. How the hell are ya'? Still seein' that skinny blond?"

"Jus' saw her a few minutes ago, cute as ever. I could use your help. I've got a bad feeling about a case I'm workin' on."

He told him about the Sheik, the black van, and the KAVU truck parked right behind it. "Maybe one of your guys saw the license plate?" Winchell reviewed the logs, found the clinic, and punched the intercom. "Hey Ricky, come to my office."

Richard was one of these certified "techies" who loved his computers as much as his girlfriend (and he absolutely worshipped his girlfriend).

His neatly braided long brown hair and his John Lennon glasses clashed with the stud in his ear and the ring through his eyebrow. His I.Q. was way off the charts. He strolled into the station manager's office and sat down next to Francisco on the couch.

"Sup, man? I'm Richard."

"We just have a few questions for you. You've done nothing wrong."

"I didn't think so. I usually know when I screw up." They asked if he recalled a flat black van parked in front of his truck at the clinic that day.

"Couldn't miss it. It was so totally loaded. It hummed. I figured it was CIA or something."

"Can you describe it? Did you get a look inside?"

"Well, it had like these major antennas and a way cool satellite dish. Way cooler than ours. Sorry boss. The tinted windows were so totally out of place. The body was all welded, no bolts and no screws. The tires were more like you'd see on a sports car. I think it was some sort of souped-up customized Chevy conversion machine."

"Did you get a look at the plate?" said Francisco, knowing it was a long shot. "Think hard. Do you remember any numbers or letters? Or even the state?"

"Duh, like I'd remember? But since it was the coolest thing I'd ever seen, I took a picture of it through my windshield. Then, I walked over to the park and took a few more. My Linda loves cool cars, and spy stuff. James Bond's Austin Martin; that guy on T.V. who talks to his car; the Batmobile, ya know? She's really into it. She put the van's pictures into her collection."

That was just the break Francisco needed. He followed Richard home, and parked in the driveway of his late 1930's bungalow. Carved pumpkins still lingered from Halloween.

"My Linda's so totally into this holiday fad stuff. In a few days there'll be pilgrims and turkeys. A week after that? Snow flakes and reindeer."

Francisco smiled and admired the house. He had spent time eating dirt in the trenches of Europe, and this place was right out of the movies he'd watched overseas. He envisioned some guy walking in saying: "Honey, I'm home", and his gal greeting him in an apron, with a kiss on the cheek, and a warm dinner on the table. The detective thought to himself, "Man, how I just love this house."

They walked up to the kitchen. Its door was wide open. Richard looked puzzled. Francisco whispered for Richard to hand him his shoe, and he signaled him to stand back. He took out his gun, stood beside the door, and tossed in the shoe. They both hit the ground as a rapid-fire weapon was emptied in their direction.

Francisco fired twice, ran in and chased a ghost out the back of the house. The assailant was climbing the six-foot wooden fence. Francisco fired two more shots. A short swarthy corpse slithered his way to the ground, leaving smudged streaks of smeared blood on the grayed cedar fence. Something was clutched in the dead man's cold hand.

Francisco approached the body, and noted an envelope. He bent down, snatched up the parcel, ripped it open and smiled. Starring at him was a negative strip and two 5x7 prints of a black Chevy van. Its New Jersey plate was blurred, but at least it was something.

"Hey Richard," yelled Francisco. "Couldn't you focus that camera of yours?"

When nobody answered, he went back inside and wandered around

Richard's ransacked cottage. Through the walls he heard wailing moans. Francisco followed the sounds into the bedroom where he found Linda's lifeless body in Richard's arms. Her throat had been slashed. So had Richard's heart.

The detective placed his hands on Richard's shoulders, who pushed them away, rocked Linda's body, and said: "Why? What have you done?"

Francisco stood silently for a moment, and then went to the kitchen and phoned the police. When the squad cars arrived, the detective got into his truck. With blurred teary eyes and a lump in his throat he drove off. He stared at his rearview mirror as the dreary gray cottage faded away.

20

No Parking Zone

Canopied beneath a brisk clear blue sky, Carole, Ha-med and Aneesa negotiated airport traffic on the busiest travel day of the year – the day before Thanksgiving. The terminal was packed tighter than an overstuffed suitcase. The loud muffled rumbles of welcome home greetings were superimposed on the hum of jet engines.

Carole's sons were due to arrive any moment. Anxiously, Aneesa looked up at Carole.

"Let's see … Eastman, Yale … Eastman, Yale. Andrew is the musician and likes to joke around. David is the doctor and he's the serious type."

Ha-med propped her up on his shoulders and Carole held his hand and her purse as they shuffled their way through the crowd.

It was the season for giving, for merchants, for shoppers, and for well-weathered con men and talented thieves. There were shaven-head gurus with flowers for sale mixed with pickpocket-pros out for a night on the town.

Security checkpoints were overwhelmed with too many travelers and not enough guards. The occasional frisking was only for show. As often as not when a metal detector sounded, security would give a cursory once-over before waving a passenger on through.

Carole squeezed Ha-med's hand and waved to Andrew, who was holding hands with the girl he'd brought home. In her other hand, she held a violin case. After hugs and kisses, he said: "Mom, meet Sarah. Sarah, meet Mom."

"Pleased to meet you, Sarah. I'd like you to meet Mr. Muhammed

Hassan, and this little jumping bean is Aneesa."

The group headed over to a coffee counter and chatted, while waiting for David's flight to arrive. They had plenty of time for introductions since the flight was running an hour behind. When they heard David's flight announced overhead, they hustled over to the gate and watched the plane empty with no sign of David. They went up to the desk and were told he'd been bumped and wouldn't arrive until the next morning at nine.

Disappointed but smiling they picked up the luggage and headed for home. Aneesa the chatterbox entertained Andrew and Sarah in the back seat.

"So, Sarah, are you his girlfriend or something?" asked Aneesa.

"Well, I am his friend, and I am a girl, so I guess you could say that."

"Andrew, how would you like a sweet little sister like me?"

By the time they arrived at the Meyer's Home, Aneesa was fast asleep on Andrew's lap. As they pulled into the driveway, Sarah was overwhelmed. Her eyes opened wide as she whispered into Andrew's ear, "Tell me you live here."

Sarah had grown up in a small apartment in Queens. Her mother kept house and her father sold insurance. A gifted musician, she'd struggled through college on scholarships, loans, and summertime jobs.

Ha-med parked his SUV in front of the house. Andrew and Sarah carried Aneesa, Ha-med took the bags and Carole grabbed the keys. Together they walked up to the door without noticing the strange dark truck parked alongside the detached garage. As Carole reached for the doorknob, an unexpected face popped out from the shadows. Their hearts stopped, then pounded as Aneesa was startled and gave out a shriek.

"Pardon the intrusion," said Detective Francisco to Ha-med, "but I need to speak with you right away."

When their pulses slowed down, they all took deep breaths and went inside. As the detective admired the lavish surroundings, Sarah and Aneesa went to the kitchen for a snack. Carole and Ha-med filled in Andrew on the Sheik and the riots.

"Maybe Sarah and I should go join David? Wherever he

is," said Andrew.

Ha-med, Andrew and Carole sat down on the couch. Francisco paced. "Nice shack," he said.

He then handed a picture of the black van to Ha-med.

"Does this look familiar?"

"Where did you get hold of this?"

The detective proceeded to tell them about Richard and Linda.

"At least now we have a lead, but watch your backs, it already cost one woman her life. I'll make sure a squad car stays close to this castle ... and Ms. Meyer, have you made your donation to the Detective's Foundation yet this year?"

Thanksgiving morning shone brightly on the estate beneath a sheltering shadow of century-old oaks. It was time to pick up David from the airport. Carole, Aneesa, and Sarah stayed home and prepared the house for Thanksgiving as Ha-med and Andrew headed back to LaGuardia. As they pulled out of the driveway, the patrolman guarding the gate waved from his car and two maids strolled in to help prepare the feast.

At the baggage claim Andrew jumped out of the car, and Ha-med drove around in hypnotic circles. He felt his eyes closing. His chin hit his chest and he jerked up his head. On Thanksgiving Day, the airport was quiet. He pulled over, and ignoring the "No stopping or standing" sign, leaned against the window, resting his weary eyes. He was shaken by a startling knock on the glass. He looked up and there was a policeman gazing suspiciously.

"OK buddy, this ain't no motel. Lets see some ID."

"Yes sir. I'm just waiting a minute to ... "

"Don't you read English? Or do you read at all?"

As Ha-med was reaching for his wallet, the officer noticed a suspicious black violin case peaking out from behind the seat. He stepped back and pulled out his gun.

"Hands on the wheel, if you move them, you're a dead man."

In a matter of seconds the car was surrounded. Ha-med was pinned down on the hood with his hands restrained behind his back as they read his name off the driver's license,

"So, Muhammed Hassan ... All by yourself at the airport with a fancy car, a black case and no ticket."

They took out the case and cautiously unlatched it at arms length then slowly opened it to find a beautiful violin. The officers found the whole scene quite amusing, but somehow the humor escaped Ha-med. Laughing, the officers walked away.

As he caught his breath another abrupt knock startled him, but this time it was followed by the warm smiles of David and Andrew. The leisurely cruise home gave them time to get acquainted. They told him that Mother thought they were leaving on Sunday morning, but they both planned to surprise her by sticking around an extra day to help at the annual Cohen Clinic Charity Lunch.

Meanwhile, Francisco kept hitting dead ends trying to find out who owned the black van. He drove into Jersey, stopping at every truck dealer in town. They were all closed for Thanksgiving, but each had a small "In case of emergency" number posted on their doors. He tracked down every owner and described the van, but no one was any help.

On a bustling street teeming with car dealerships was a Thanksgiving party on a custom truck lot. The lively crowd was drinking, munching, and dancing away. No one noticed Francisco stroll past the band, the kegs and the grill overflowing with hot turkey legs.

He grabbed a turkey leg, and danced his way to the middle of the bash in Chevy's Custom Van parking lot. He tried in vain to get someone's attention.

Losing his patience, he grabbed a mic from the band and while displaying his badge and his gun, he screamed at the top of his lungs, "Which one of you is Chevy?"

"Who wants to know?" said a pleasantly round fifty-ish year old man in a turkey costume.

"A tired, cranky, frustrated detective with a badge and a gun."

The owner removed his mask, and Francisco showed him the photographs, and said, "Who could make something like this?"

"Follow me, and by the way, no one here is named Chevy. That's an abbreviation for Chevrolet, y'know? A car company? I'm Jerry. I own the place. What's this all about?"

"Some guy driving around town in this thing likes killing people who take pictures of it. Who might know where I could find it?" said Francisco.

He followed Jerry to an office. The humming computers and twinkling keyboards made Francisco's blood pressure rise. He suffered from technophobia, and computers scared him to death. Jerry sat down at the keyboard and punched away like a maestro composing a tune. He printed out a name, an address, and handed it to the detective.

"This is the guy you're lookin' for. If he didn't build it, he'd know who did. William Kennedy Wallace, they call him Billy. He used to work for the government, but now his skills go to the highest bidder. Rich mafiosos, millionaire rock stars, paranoid oil tycoons, you know the type. He can take a Model T and turn it into a Sherman tank."

"Thanks, here's my card. I owe you one," said the Detective. "If you're ever in a bind, gimme a call. Happy Thanksgiving."

As Francisco strolled out, he wondered what Billy could do for his beat up old truck. He headed off to an upscale Staten Island neighborhood to ask him in person. He drove up to the little Italiante Villa. The circular drive was blocked by a black Porsche, a customized Hummer, and an overdressed Harley. He parked out front and strolled between candlestick cypress trees lining the walkway. The deafening stereo overpowered the doorbell.

He pounded on the door. No luck. He tried the doorknob, it was locked. He got up on his tiptoes, and in full stretch, reached above the doorframe. To his surprise, he found dust, but no key. He walked around back through the wrought iron gate and lifted the mat by the door to the kitchen. He smiled, lifted the key, and let himself in while yelling over the blaring music. "Hello? Anyone home?"

Cold pizza and warm beer coated the counter tops. He eased his way further and turned into the living room with his gun drawn. A massive cabinet with a stereo inside came crashing down towards him. The earsplitting noise took an impromptu rest. A growling German Shepard appeared whose snarling gave way to mutters and whines as he licked blood from his paw. Francisco backed away and the dog followed him to the kitchen. He took some warm water and soap, kneeled down and cleaned off his paw. Francisco followed him to Billy – who was dangling from a noose slung above the upstairs landing.

His neck was broken.

Detective Francisco was leaving a trail of dead people and William K. Wallace was no help at all.

When the police cars arrived, Francisco left with the dog. He posed on the Harley, glanced at the Hummer, stopped at the Porsche and drove off in his trusty old Ford. He stared at the photograph of the van with a New Jersey License Plate. It was blurry, but he managed to decipher a couple of letters. As the clock ticked away, he had an idea.

He floored the gas and flew back to Richard's. He tapped on the storm door and when Richard saw who it was, he slammed the inside door.

"Don't you want to know who murdered your girl?"

"I assume it was the guy who left his blood on my fence."

"That guy's just a pawn in some terrorists chess match. So was Linda. So are we. If we don't check-mate the King, more pawns will fall."

He let Francisco in, and the dog tagged close behind.

"So, ya wanna help, or not?"

"Maybe. Depends on what you're thinking. I'm afraid to ask."

"See the license plate on this picture? Ya think you can clean it up a little?"

"At least give me something challenging." He scanned the photo and zoomed in on the license plate. In seconds, it was enlarged, enhanced, digitalized, and focused. The numbers were crystal clear. Francisco pulled up a chair and sat beside Richard with a hound dog expression on his boxer-like face.

"Sorry I kinda ran out of here, sorry about Linda, sorry for your loss." Francisco sighed, leaned back, and continued in an out-of-character paternal tone. "Twenty-five years ago I tore apart a skinhead neo-Nazi psycho for burning down a church. When they hauled him away he looked me in the eye, spit in my face and called me a nigger-loving wetback.

My wife was about to turn 25 when he got paroled. I came home one night, and found her with a slit throat. He was still in the house. I shot him six times."

The teary-eyed men stared into space and the dog whimpered.

"OK, 'nuff said. How's this for a challenge: Hack your way into the motor vehicle bureau files and find out who owns the van."

Richard's interest was sparked.

"Now we're talking," he said. He lifted a dust cover off of a console where computers and screens and two keyboards in tandem sat mourning Linda's death.

Francisco's hands rested on Richard's shoulders as he watched his fingers waltzing in vain. Over and over the screens kept on saying: "You do not have clearance" and "ACCESS DENIED."

"I'm goin' to Jersey. Call me if you get something. Wouldja' keep an eye on Dawg for me?"

They shook hands, and Francisco walked out the door, got into his truck, cranked up the engine and as he was driving off, he saw the screen door fly open. Richard was yelling and Dawg was barking.

"Access Granted. We got it. We're in!"

Richard ran out and handed a printout to Francisco. The address was a warehouse in Newark, New Jersey, owned by an Islamic Educational Foundation whose president was Dr. Emit Dahij. He couldn't thank Richard enough. "When this case is over, how 'bout you teach me something about computers?"

As Detective Francisco drove back to New Jersey, the Ibrahims drove past the police car guarding Ms. Meyer's home. With mutual expressions of total amazement they parked in the crowded driveway and walked to the door where smiling Aneesa greeted them. After introducing them to the crowd she gave them a tour.

Ha-med, Carole, Sheryl, Saul and his wife, Mr. And Mrs. McDaniel, the boys and Sarah were seated in the living room enjoying the aroma of fresh pecan from the fireplace while snacking on delicacies and sipping hot cider. Dr. Brennen's husband and son assisted her as she waddled behind her very pregnant belly, afraid that if she sat down, she might never get up.

After their tour, the Ibrahims joined the rest of the crowd. A few moments later, Aneesa strolled in giggling and ringing a dainty crystal bell. "Dinner is now served. Would you please follow me to the dining hall."

The dining room scene was right out of King Henry VIII. They wined and they dined and talked about life. Everyone agreed to be at the clinic on Sunday to help feed those less fortunate folks. The table was cleared and the maids brought out coffee, ice cream and a huge pecan pie from Saul's.

A black limousine pulled up to the gate; the chauffer rolled down his tinted window as the police officer approached and requested I.D. A few moments later Carole's phone rang, and the maid answered it. She walked up behind Carole and whispered. "A tall, darkly dressed man with a big hat is at the door. He asked if he might stop in to wish you and Mr. Hassan well – says his name is Kahane."

Carole went to the door and invited Mr. Kahane in with a warm loving hug. They entered the dining room, Ha-med stood up, and the two men shook hands and sat down. Kahane had a bag with him that he emptied out on the table: a napkin, kosher cake, silverware and a bottle of wine. Aneesa walked right up to him, and stared him up and down.

"Hello Sir, Happy Thanksgiving. My name is Aneesa. Why did you bring a sack lunch? We have plenty of food. How come you dress funny, and wear a big hat? Why do you keep your hair long on the sides? And what are those strings hanging out the back of your shirt?"

A deafening hush silenced the room. He looked down and saw her huge innocent eyes. He tickled her belly, pinched her cheek, sat her on his lap and proceeded to explain his strange customs to her.

Ha-med Hassan stood up and proposed a toast. They all raised their glasses.

"We are all of a common God, He who put Abraham to the ultimate test. Would he kill in the name of Allah? He would. He failed. God was telling us something. No one can murder and blame it on God. Not even Abraham. As terrorists attempt to suck us into their web, they hide behind false veils of, "God told us to." May someday we see a ceasefire of terror; turn swords into plow shears and know war no more. On Thanksgiving we give thanks that our hardships are few, and we pray that our joys are too numerous to count."

The air filled with sounds of Lechaiyim, Salud, Cheers, and Slainte.

21

Cousins

For Felix Francisco, Thanksgiving Dinner consisted of a hot dog and pretzel while driving across the bridge into New Jersey and wondering where this Dr. Dahij fit in. He looked at the beady-eyed, scruffy-bearded photo staring at him from the passenger seat as he approached the Port of Newark. He searched for a warehouse hoping it housed a one-handed sheik in a black custom van.

Nighttime had fallen on the slick icy docks and a cold drizzle lurked behind Francisco's back. He parked by a rusted, rat-infested dumpster and snooped around the heavily bolted sliding steel door, which posted an unambiguous sign: "Private, Keep Out."

He snuck around back, cleared the fog from the thick steel-reinforced window glass and peered into a dark empty room. With the butt of his gun he tried fruitlessly to break the window. With mounting frustration he stood back, fired two shots, and through the shattered glass he pried open the latch.

He muscled his way up, squeezed himself through, and eased his feet down on the cold concrete floor. The sickening stench of fresh paint, decaying harbor trash, salty diesel ships and a hint of sulfur filled the room. He took a cigarette lighter from his pocket, illuminated his path, and while sticking to oil and tripping on tools he flipped on a switch. The flickering hum of fluorescent lights unveiled an auto workshop. No van and no Sheik, just a cold vacant warehouse.

He rode the elevator upstairs and sat himself down behind a desk. The seat was still warm. A broken pencil, a pad, a small pile of fresh ashes, envelopes and stationary sat on the desktop. He picked up half a pencil and rubbed its side on a blank writing pad. A neatly inscribed silhouetted outline appeared, bearing the name "Emit Dahij".

Beneath it was an erratically scribbled message: "When the upright and fallen come together, you will witness the guilty on that day linked together in chains. The names of the righteous are mirrored reflections whose evil sides hide in their minds eyes and words."

Francisco scratched his head and stuffed the note into his pocket. His next stop was the Newark Police Station. He flashed them his badge and they welcomed him in. They searched the criminal files but found no record of Ahmed Muhammed Khalil or Emit Dahij. They accessed the files of commercial properties at the docks.

"Emit Dahij sure owns that old warehouse, under the name "The Dahij Foundation for Religious Unity," said the Police Chief. "No evidence of criminal activity associated with it. He plans to convert it into some sort of school or something."

Francisco was chasing his tail.

No Sheik, no van, and Dahij's name keeps popping up.

He thanked the chief, and drove aimlessly down a brightly lit street. There were clubs, discos, bars, a strip joint, Internet cafes, and some cheap motels. He checked into a motel, jumped into a warm shower and tried to fit the pieces together in his mind: the Sheik, the van at the Cohen Clinic, the Dahij Foundation and the abandoned warehouse. He remembered something the Imam had told him ... a mosque in New Jersey had first contacted him regarding Sheik Ahmed Muhammed Khalil. He dried off and remembered the name of a club down the street. He picked up the phone, and punched four one-one.

"This is Detective Francisco. Can you please connect me with the *World Wide Web Café* in Newark?"

"Certainly detective, one moment please." After several rings, a sweet young female voice struggled to compete with the clanking of bottles, atonal loud music, and the laughter of crowds.

"Three W Café, can I help you?"

"Is this a place I could learn how to use the Internet?"

"That's all we do here honey. Twenty-four seven, we're always on line."

Francisco drove down the street into a parking lot packed with young techies and chicks. He walked in the door and immediately recognized the voice he had heard on the phone.

"This ain't no line, Hon," said Francisco. " I really need your help. I've never done this before ... Computers scare me to death."

This babe about thirty had short red spiked hair, a ring through her navel, and one through her brow. Her skin-tight shirt flaunted her nipple-pierced breasts.

"If she'd lose all that hardware, grow out her hair and put on a bra, she'd be hot," Detective Francisco thought to himself.

"My name's Francisco. I spoke with you on the phone."

"Hi. I'm Rayne," she said gripping his outstretched hand with a surprisingly strong handshake. "Yep, sounds like rain, but it's spelled R-A-Y-N-E. My hippie parents thought it was cute. It was raining one night thirty years ago, and they got stranded in the back seat of their car, so here I am. I'd be glad to help you out."

He ordered a pizza and a large pot of coffee and the next thing he knew he had an email address and was surfing the web. Francisco looked her in the eyes with as unintentionally mischievous smile.

"I'm a detective, on a very dangerous mission."

He paused, moved a little closer, and whispered in her ear, "I'm searching for an Arab Sheik and his black van."

"Yeah, right. And I'm a virgin. Let's see your badge, Mr. Bond."

When he pulled out his badge, her jaw hit the tabletop. Her face turned bright red. The two started laughing and got back to work. For over an hour they tried numerous search engines, typing in "sheik," "mosque," "Khalil," "Dahij," "New Jersey," "Long Island" – anything that came to mind.

Websites galore mentioned Sheik Ahmed Khalil. From one such site they were able to print out a grainy black and white photo of him. He was an imposing figure with his face in the shadows.

His villainous reputation was scary. Terrorist pages sang songs of his praises while legitimate Mosques banned him from showing his face.

Emit Dahij was widely admired and respected. His personal website spoke only of peace. Francisco put his palms gently on each of Rayne's temples, and planted a big kiss on her forehead.

"Darlin', I owe you one. How can I thank you?"

"Hey detective," said Rayne, who smiled and continued, "Got any handcuffs to go with that badge?"

As Francisco's face was now bright red, she continued.

"Gotcha! Just kidding. If you get a computer, here's my e-mail address."

He thanked her again, and headed back to his motel room. He leaned back on a squeaky old recliner and closed his eyes just for a moment. The next thing he heard was the rumbling of semis hitting the road at daybreak. He cruised back to his station and sat at his desk behind a stack of old papers, cold coffee and stale Krispy Kremes. He ate a hard donut, and called the Imam.

"I spent some time last night surfin' the web. This Sheik is bad news."

"I also have some troubling information," said the Imam. "I called a Mosque in New Jersey, the one that asked me if the Sheik could visit us. I was deceived ... a con job. They never called. They didn't even know he was in town. He was banned from their mosque years ago. So, I checked the phone records. The calls were long distance, from a mosque in London."

"Tell me something else Imam. Ever hear of some guy, some professor named Dahij?" said Francisco.

"Sure. He lectures all over the world, but his popularity is not what it once was. He studied here in the sixties, y'know? During the hippie years."

Two polite knocks on the detective's door startled him. He lost his train of thought, ignored the knocking and continued. So, what about this Dahij?"

Detective Francisco had completely forgotten. He was to break in a fresh recruit – a top-notch police cadet who had been assigned to help him with this case, and was due to arrive that day.

Top of the class from the academy, the fastest, the brightest, and the best with a gun.

But it was bad timing; the detective was in no mood for rookies.

This time, three knocks pounded on his door.

"I'm busy, get lost for a while."

"Are you still there?" asked the Imam.

Just when Francisco thought he made his point, his intercom buzzed and the desk clerk said: "Your 'junior detective' is here, and is really anxious to get started."

"I'll call you right back," said Francisco to the Imam as three more knocks hammered away in rapid succession. He hung up the phone and yelled. "I'm not deaf. Just open the damn door and come the hell in!"

The door opened, and in strutted the rookie.

Francisco sat mesmerized.

She stood five-foot eight with gorgeous blue eyes and a flawless face.

The sleep-deprived detective tried hard not to notice how nicely her uniform clung to her thighs.

She gave a perfect salute.

"Officer Landry, reporting for duty, sir."

Francisco stood up, his thighs hit the desk, and a cup of cold coffee spilled on his lap.

"At ease," he said, while wiping his lap. "Welcome to work, glad to have you on board."

"Thank you, sir. There is a tall, soft-spoken foreigner sitting in the lobby waiting to see you. He has a Middle Eastern accent, and a leather-bound book in his hand. He asked me to give you this card."

She handed him the card.

Francisco's weary eyes strained to make out the fine print.

"Doctor Emit Dahij, Professor of Islamic Studies, and Proprietor of Fine Muslim Books and Antiques. Haifa, Israel. New Jersey, USA."

Detective Francisco's blood-shot eyes opened wide as he tried to compose himself, and asked Landry to show him in. A clean-shaven man in a fine, three-piece suit and wire-rimmed glasses followed her in. In his hand was a magnificent Koran. The three sat down, and after brief introductions, Dahij began to speak.

"I landed in Newark, and drove straight to my building, a building that will soon be a temple, a church, a mosque.

"A house of worship to welcome those of all faiths. I cringed as I entered. It has been ransacked and burglarized. I purchased a bulletproof van at a government auction. It was gone. I investigated inquiries on my web page, and noticed several from an interesting location: an Internet café in New Jersey. So I visited the café and a strange looking girl named Rayne said you were looking for me. So, here I am. How can I be of service?"

The Koran captivated Officer Landry. "That book is just fabulous. May I take a closer look?"

Dahij would not let go.

"This is one of only two copies. They are the oldest known to man. The pair was handwritten by a scribe who witnessed Muhammed rise to the heavens."

This beautiful woman knew beautiful things. The leather was fine-tooled with gold inlaid letters and its contents were adorned by magnificent hand-colored art.

Detective Francisco asked Dahij: "So, you say there's another copy. Where is it?"

Dahij clasped his hands, closed his eyes, and spoke from his heart. "His name is Sheik Ahmed Muhammed Khalil. I will now share with you in confidence what few have been privileged to know. Our fathers were identical twins. Ahmed is my cousin. We too are difficult to tell apart."

Detective Francisco and Officer Landry sat back and listened to this gifted storyteller convey the legend of Emit and the Sheik ...

> *A long time ago in a land far away lived a simple young woman. She spent her time working the fields for some farmers, as did her parents before her, and their parents before them. When she'd view her reflection upon the still waters it made her tears flow and her heart became hollow. In sorrow her hands tossed pebbles upon it so ripples would blur the plain image she saw. When currents ceased, the same face would return. She looked towards the heavens and prayed to Allah.*
>
> *"I ask not for years to help blot away tears. I ask not for wealth, nor for immortal health. I seek no possessions; I resist man's transgressions. I live simple and plain, yet I*

wander in pain. As my days slowly fade, Allah, grant my one prayer: that my beauty may blossom. Let this maiden be fair."

Allah looked down on this woman in pity, knowing her wish was a double-edged sword. On the day she turned thirty she sat by a spring and a wise weeping willow wept by her side. This immense ancient tree had a story as well. A long time ago this young tree gazed around her, admiring the beauty in all of God's gifts. With whispers of wisdom it grew proud and stood tall. In its youth, it was simple and off to its right sprung the most beautiful glorious flowering bush. Her glowing green leaves and bright flowers of gold were admired, not envied by this plain looking tree. The insects and beavers and birds all adored it. The attention they gave it at first made it shine, but soon this sad shrub needed rest from the crowds who fought over it until it withered and died.

Allah had given this woman a warning as she drifted to sleep beneath the wise willow tree. A fever had placed her on the doorstep of death as she slept for three days without water or food. Adverse visions soon drove her insane. She envisioned two men with one face in a struggle, dueling each other till just one survived. One wore bright white, while the other bore black. An angel from Allah whispered in her ear.

"If it is beauty you wish for, you must pay a price. Many suitors will want you. Your splendor will lure them like bees drawn to honey; like flowers to sun. They will offer you gifts and desire to know you and you may know all, but may never choose one. As you awake, if you stare into the pond, your wish will be granted, your plain life disposed. If you choose to be humble; content with simplicity, pass by the water with eyes tightly closed."

When she awoke she glanced into the pond and stared in delight at her magnificence. As her days passed by she was courted by many. Kings, sheiks and princes flocked to her fields. They'd wine her, and dine her, and she knew them all.

A jealous King wanted her all to himself, and one night he got down on his knees and he begged. The answer she gave him (like all those before him) was cruel but she knew that she had to decline. His moments without her would torment his soul. He kissed her sweet lips as he went off to battle; his nightmares were plagued knowing she was not his.

What he had not known was that during his absence she had given birth to his twin sons. From the day they were born one was praised; one was scorned. All who saw them together could tell them apart. Though identical twins, one was meek; one was twisted. The king never knew his two children existed.

On the day he returned, his love for her burned him as flames of desire singed holes in his heart. The evening turned nighttime, and night turned to dawn. As he viewed her rare beauty and watched her lay sleeping he knew he could not bear to share her again. When the sun's morning shine gave her breasts a warm glow, he asked her one more time to love only him. With tears in her eyes she told him her sad story. In his insane passion, he loved her yet killed her and then took his knife to his own broken heart.

The dead woman's vanity lead to insanity and a seed from each orphan gave rise to a son. Ahmed was satanic while Emit was pure and they maintained their distance for fear of a war.

Francisco and Landry had hypnotic stares as Dahij spoke.

"I wish I knew where my coiled snake cousin hides, waiting to strike at my neck."

Detective Francisco called the Imam, Ha-med, Mr. Ibrahim, and Afridi and they set up a meeting with Dr. Dahij at the mosque at a quarter to five.

22

"I do!"

On the day after Thanksgiving, as most people were either resting at home or holiday shopping, an inconspicuous white-and-orange rental truck cruised along the quiet Newark streets.

Who'd ever guess that it was hauling a two-thousand pound bomb disguised as an ambulance?

The truck turned down a peaceful dirt road and entered a desolate, frost-covered field. It pulled over.

The Sheik emerged, followed by two others, and proudly watched as they hauled down the loading ramp and rolled out the sparkling red ambulance. The Sheik got behind the wheel and cruised around town like a kid in his new shinny car. He tapped on the horn as he passed by the police station and they smiled and waved. He pulled into a drive-through just for fun, ordered a shake and returned to the field. He drove up the ramp, stepped out on the platform, opened his cherished Koran with his crippled hand, and recited his favorite verse:

"Seize them and kill them wherever you find them, and take not from among them a helper or friend."

They heaved up the ramp, and with a resounding crash let the door down and locked it. They drove to an old fire station on Long Island whose hooks and ladders were long gone. It had been converted to a party hall for rent and for the long holiday weekend, it belonged to the Sheik.

They opened the massive old firehouse door, backed in next to a shinny black Corvette and let the door come crashing down. The vast hollow space had cinderblock walls, a smooth concrete floor, a huge metal roof and two large metal doors. When the Sheik started preaching, the roof began creaking. His words filled the room and they oozed out the chimney and echoed with psychotic satanic hate. He tossed Corvette keys to one of his brainwashed soldiers, then handed him a cache of cash. It was the same crispy bills that were given to Billy, but he no longer had any use for them.

"You have been chosen to join those in paradise as you deliver God's gift to the infidels," wailed the Sheik to his sacrificial driver. "Get your hair groomed, and part with your beard. Anoint your skin with the finest cologne. Select fine garments of silk and dress as they do."

The Sheik paused, slouched and whispered, "When darkness falls, you shall gather man's sins and repel his indiscretions. Intoxicate yourself and dwell with young whores in their clubs and their bars and their parks and their homes."

He soared to full height with his hands in the air and echoed in a resounding vibrato.

"Seduce them and fill them with your lustful seeds, and seek out young men as you hasten God's plague. Return to me Sunday at sunrise as we bow and pray. Your reward awaits you for your righteous transgressions."

The Sheik stared out into space in a trance. He raised his trembling hands even higher, clutching his Koran. He eyes were fixed on his violently twitching crippled hand. His quivering voice began speaking in nonsensical tongues like a stark raving madman. He fell to the ground, writhing uncontrollably, never letting go of his sacred Koran.

He lay still for a moment then rose to his feet as if nothing had happened. His frightened disciples stood frozen with fear as his preaching continued in a soft tranquil tone.

"May Allah be pleased with your actions and deeds as young luscious virgins await your arrival."

At the Meyer home, the maids were busy cleaning as the guests began to wake at twenty past ten on this lazy overcast November morning. Sarah, Andrew, David, Aneesa, Ms. Meyer and Ha-med converged on the kitchen and found biscuits in the oven, fresh juice on the table, hot cocoa for Aneesa and coffee on the stove. The soothing aroma of logs on the fire filled the air with warmth and their hearts with thanksgiving.

After a snack they showered and dressed, then cuddled close by the fire with coffee in hand.

Aneesa looked around at the lazy crowd.

"You guys are boring me to death. Doesn't any one want to do anything?"

The relaxing group looked around at each other, hoping for a volunteer.

There was a harmonious sigh of relief when Andrew said, "Hey Aneesa, how 'bout you and I show Sarah the duck pond?"

Before he completed his sentence, Aneesa was bundled up, ready to go and whispered to Andrew.

"Ask Mom if we can take her car."

As they approached the park, Aneesa told them all about her last trip there and how she introduced her father to Carole. They parked, walked over to the pond and tossed in some bread. While Aneesa continued feeding the ducks, Andrew and Sarah sat behind her on a bench. When Aneesa saw them cuddling and kissing she turned and walked over.

"Those poor ducks must be cold, the water looks freezing. You two sure look warm and cozy. I think I need a boyfriend."

Andrew lifted her up and wedged her between he and Sarah. "If any guys ever bother you," said Andrew, "They'll have to answer to me."

The park was peaceful and calm. Aneesa noticed a man sitting alone on a bench with a book and a briefcase. She jumped down and walked up to him under Andrew's watchful eye.

"Happy Thanksgiving, Sir. I'm Aneesa, and I'm five."

The man answered in a thick foreign accent. "Aneesa is a very pretty name. Did you know that it means *friend*?"

"Yes. It's Arabic. My parents are Arabic, but my mother died." They continued to chat. Andrew and Sarah came over and she introduced them. "And kind sir," Aneesa asked, "What is *your* name?"

He stood up and nodded his head in a dignified fashion. "I am Dr.

Emit Dahij, but you may call me Emit," he said while offering his hand.

"Please to meet you, Dr. Dahij," said Aneesa, while curtsying and eyeing his Koran. "That is a very pretty Koran. May I see it?"

He would not let it out of his hands, but they all sat on the bench as he skimmed through it, demonstrating the magnificent artwork.

"My father has one that looks kinda like yours, but his is newer, and the colors are brighter," said Aneesa. Dahij grinned, knowing that her father's was one of the many reproductions. "This one is centuries old, but I'm sure your father's carries the same teachings and is equally beautiful."

"What does the Koran say about choosing a spouse?" asked Andrew, as Sarah blushed. "What's a spouse?" asked Aneesa.

The wise aged man said: "Aneesa, a spouse is a mate, and a special friend with whom you form a precious alloy."

"What's an alloy?"

"It's when two metals are kinda melted together," said Sarah.

"Oh, you mean like two people hugging, I get it."

Dahij flipped through the pages, stood, and faced Andrew.

"The translation from ancient Aramaic to English is a bit tricky, but what Muhammed has told us is that we cannot guide whom we love, but Allah guides whom He pleases, and knows best the followers of the right way. We are also told that men and women are each other's halves, like twins."

The group sat and talked a little longer, then Emit said, "I thank Allah for bringing us together today, and allowing us to enjoy one another's company. If Allah wills it, I shall be fortunate enough to cross your paths again."

"Next time I see you, may I hold your Koran?" asked Aneesa.

"We shall see, little angel, little friend, we shall see."

In his rented Ford Taurus, Emit drove to the mosque and both Ha-med and Momar drove up as he parked.

Ha-med shook his hand and bowed his head.

"During my studies in Paris I had the pleasure of attending one of your lectures, I again heard you speak several years ago during my first visit to New York. A rude heckler was dragged out by security." Dahij smiled, but Ha-med could not tell if he remembered or not.

"These days too many young people find refuge in those who yell the loudest, while twisting Muhammed's words and Allah's commands!" said Dahij.

The three of them nodded their heads in agreement and a soothing silence filled the air. The mood was invaded by squeaking brakes, a clamoring engine and clunking fenders. The beat up ford truck hit the curb as it parked. Detective Francisco got out, then Landry slid over and got out as well.

The Imam welcomed them inside and they assembled in his study. Ha-med, Momar, Afridi, Francisco, Landry and the Imam thanked the professor for volunteering his time and offering advice. They went around the room brainstorming. Landry took notes on a yellow legal pad.

"The Sheik was first seen here a few weeks ago," said the Imam.

"My black van? It just vanished?" said Dahij.

"He left for a while. Then he returned," said Ha-med.

"Where is he now?" said Afridi.

"He's bad news!" said Momar.

"He ransacked my warehouse and now has a bulletproof van!" said Dahij.

Francisco remembered the note in his pocket.

"I traced this off a pad on your desk at the warehouse," said the detective as he handed the note to Dahij, and continued.

"From the looks of it, whoever wrote it was mad. The strokes are sloppy yet bold; the impression is strong, violent looking. Whoever it was broke the pencil, and there were ashes on the table. He may have burned the letter."

Dahij stood up and read it slowly and precisely to the group while tightly grasping his sacred Koran.

"When the upright and fallen come together, you will witness the guilty linked together in chains. The names of the righteous are mirrored reflections whose evil sides hide in their mind's eyes and words."

He handed the note back to the detective.

"A central portion of these words seems to paraphrase Muhammed. They are from the Koranic book of Abraham. Within their intended passage they provide wisdom. Taken out of context, and intermingled with gibberish, their meaning is lost. They are no doubt spoken from the heart of a troubled mind. I fear that Cousin Ahmed is planning something terrible."

It was then time for prayer, so Francisco and Landry took off.

"The first thing we do is get the bomb squad to check out the clinic," said Francisco. "On Sunday morning, we'll set up roadblocks and checkpoints." They went to the station, alerted the bomb squad, and organized a security task force of plain-clothed detectives to help serve the food and uniformed officers to patrol the grounds. The Detective and rookie drove over to the clinic, and searched the grounds with a fine-toothed comb. They strolled through the park, and sat down on the bench.

"Well?" said Francisco in an endearing tone, "How'd ya like your first day on the job?"

Landry leaned back, locked her fingers behind her head, and with a refreshing smile said, "Piece of cake."

"You did well. After we check out at the station, go home and get some rest. See ya at six a.m. Stop by for donuts on your way in."

It was Saturday afternoon at 2:30 when a white limo pulled up to the old county courthouse. The overcast sky gave way to cotton clouds against a background of crisp brilliant blue. A carpet of rusty orange leaves coated the cobblestone path from the road to the courthouse.

Ha-med got out of the limo dressed like a sultan in a white silk brocade and a sword just for show. The Ibrahims and Aneesa followed. David and Andrew escorted Carole who looked like a dream in her silky white gown with a hint of crimson. A delicate veil draped her glistening highlights of cascading golden-brown strands.

The clergy arrived in traditional robes and the beaming guests were well attired. Joy seeped out the windows and door of the small cozy chapel. Carole, Ha-med, the Ibrahims, the Rabbi and the Imam assembled beneath a huppa-like tent in front of the long narrow room. The Imam held a Koran in hand, and spoke.

"As our Prophet of Islam has told us, you cannot guide whom you are to love but Allah will guide those who will please each other. Men are told that women are our twin halves. Allah, the Supreme, God of

Abraham, Moses, Jesus, and Muhammed, smiles today upon Carole and Ha-med and displays before us a guiding light of shared thoughts."

The Imam paused, and looked toward Ha-med.

"Ha-med, our prophet has said that the most precious gift Allah can give you is a virtuous wife who you look at with pleasure. Now go and become each other's finest garments."

The Imam took one step back, and the Rabbi stepped forward with scriptures in hand. "As God looked down upon Adam, he thought that Man should not be alone, so he made him a mate. Maimonides coined the phrase *bashert*, soul-mate. Ha-med and Carole, you are *basherteem*, soul mates. I knew it from the moment I saw you together. In Hebrew *re'im ahuvim* means loved companions and *v'ahavta l'rayacha* is to love ones neighbor. Rabbi Rashi described the love between bride and the groom as the culmination of these expressions. May God bless and protect this fine couple. May they be an example to us all."

Hand in hand, Carole and Ha-med stepped forward. Carole spoke first.

"In centuries past, Baal Shem Tov said that from each human being a light shines, reaching heaven. When two destined souls find each other and merge, a much brighter stream shines forth. He must have been thinking of me and Ha-med."

Carole looked into Ha-med's eyes and continued.

"King Solomon has told us that he, who has found woman, has found good. I'm glad that you found me."

The group beneath the huppa glanced toward the first row of seats. Aneesa was strolling with tissues in hand, blotting the tears from her Grandparents eyes.

Ha-med then spoke.

"Allah, the most Gracious speaks much about spouses. Our wives are our partners and committed helpers and we take them with God's permission and trust. They have been created so we can live life in tranquility. In his last sermon, Muhammed told us that Allah plants love and mercy between us, and nothing increases this love like a marriage. All these words just skim the surface of the love I have for Carole."

Now face to face, Carole and Ha-med exchanged this vow:

"Entreat me not to leave you, and to return from following after you; for where you go I will go. Where you lodge, I will lodge; Your People shall be my People, and your God, my God."

Aneesa approached with the rings.

To a roomful of wet eyes, they proclaimed "I do."

Ha-med leaned Carole way back, and as they were kissing, David cleared his throat, and walked up with a glass and a napkin. He wrapped the glass and placed it in front of Ha-med's right foot. With a resounding crash, his foot crushed the glass. Harmonious echoes of "*Mazel Tov!*" and "Praise Allah!" reverberated off the thick courthouse walls.

The caravan headed over to Mahshi's where the feast and festivities welcomed them in. Colorful banners and streamers adorned the walls and music filled the air as the guests filtered in.

The buffet and dessert table looked too good to be real as its cultural blend surpassed all ethnic boundaries. After traditional Arabic dances and songs, they all danced the Hora with chairs raised up high. At six o'clock sharp the new lovers were off.

They cruised to an enchanting resort in the Hamptons. A uniformed doorman welcomed them into a lobby boasting breathtaking views of the sea's soaring waves.

Arriving at the door of their suite, a tuxedoed butler greeted them. As he opened the double French doors, a sterling bowl sat there with Dom Perignon, surrounded by kiwi and grapes. He showed them around, switched on music, brought them some ice and said,

"If there will be nothing else, I shall leave you two alone."

Leaving a generous tip, Ha-med bolted the door.

They sat on a wicker bench in their enclosed glass terrace, watched the sunset then strolled back inside and he poured some champagne. Ha-med placed his strong hands on Carole's trim waist. She slipped off his coat, unbuttoned his shirt, kissed his chest and backed away into the bedroom. He chugged another glass of champagne to subdue his soaring pulse.

Ha-med heard the water running, and walked into the master bath where he found Carole in the fog, her translucent white-crimson wedding gown illuminated by flickering scented candles. She circled him and from behind massaged his neck. Without him seeing, she slipped off her gown, and then whispered while kissing his ear, "I don't know about you, but I sure need a shower."

He turned and found her clothing strewn on the floor and watched her firm naked body fade into the mist. He opened the shower and through the fog, admired the beauty of her stark silhouette.

She arched back her neck, her hair shimmered like gold. Water-beads skimmed down her breasts' firm plateaus, then skipped off her nipples like fountains in Rome.

He undressed while still gazing, and joined his new bride; they rinsed off their bodies while sipping champagne. These born again virgins with love long ignored were like wandering ivy as their bodies entwined. Their mouths and their tongues formed a boiling cauldron as their minds and their hearts became alloyed as one.

His molten lips made their way to her breasts; then slid their way down to her oozing abyss.

She sat down on the bench and thrusted herself towards his passionate mouth. She leaned herself back as he lifted her up and grabbed on to her buttocks as she cried out his name. His powerful tongue just kept plunging and slurping to her body's ecstatic gyrations of love.

She stood up and shoved Ha-med down on the bench and then teased his lips with the tip of her tongue. She slid her tongue down his chest, to his thighs, and then on her knees, she continued to tease. She dawdled until his breaths finally slowed, then burst through the mist with her tireless bobbing and synchronized efforts of her lips and her tongue. She grabbed onto his buttocks and pulled him in deeper; then paused there until he was perfectly still. She withdrew herself slowly; a millimeter at a time, then with powerful suction, pulled him in again. Her alternating roughness and gentle caress kept him right on the edge for an eternity.

She stood up, cooled the water, and they showered again. He could stand it no longer. He lifted her up, and carried her off while whispering in her ear: "You are Allah's most beautiful creation, and I am privileged to love you."

She wisped her hair to the side, and whispered,"Do you love me because I am beautiful or am I beautiful because you love me?"

As they entered the bedroom, the candlelight's flames danced in her eyes and the moonlight skimmed off the rippling ocean waves below. They stood up and merged into one melting body, the moment they dreamed of was well worth their wait.

On the verge of their mutual volcanic eruptions, the bed was too distant. They fell to the floor. Their bodies entwined in a fugue-form duet, ignoring all boundaries of mind, heart, and flesh. Loud cries and soft whispers of "Carole" and "Ha-med" unleashed rhythmic unselfish desires to please. She toppled him over, surrounding his body with a finale of powerful jackhammer thrusts. Their eyes closed and necks arched in rapturous union amidst chaotic contortions of love, lust, and need. The sounds of her ecstasy echoed then ceased as explosive pulsations filled her body with warmth.

23

The Final Chapter

Sunday sneaked up on the Charles Cohen Clinic. The light of dawn squinted, defrosting the dew beneath towering scaffolds and palettes of bricks as the nightshift of nurses were giving report to their morning replacements at six forty-five.

A huge truck with a driver and one passenger pulled up to the gate. They handed some papers to the guard. He looked them over, looked at the men within, circled once around the truck then smiled as he waved them through. They crossed the main parking lot, where later that day hundreds would feast on a Thanksgiving lunch. After parallel parking as close as they could to the main building, the driver and passenger rubbed their hands to warm them, put on gloves, got out of the truck, went around to the rear, unlocked the sliding steel door, and muscled it up and out of the way. They looked inside, took deep breaths, looked at each other and began unloading dozens of banquet tables, hundreds of folding chairs, and a massive canvas tent.

Several miles away a similar truck was preparing its contents for the same festive lunch. A clean-cut looking young man unlatched the gate and rolled up the door.

Sheik Ahmed Muhammed Khalil climbed aboard and unscrewed a panel on the side of the ambulance revealing a keypad. With his deformed index finger, he punched in "nine-one-one," and to the glow of an iridescent neon light, he smiled and replaced the panel.

A heavy iron shoebox-sized case stood at his feet. At his command, his driver lifted it up, unlatched it, took out a high-tech device resembling a cell phone and handed it to the Sheik, who entered a code.

The simple, foolproof plan required just three components: A two thousand pound bomb, a cell phone, and a madman.

When the Sheik enters "nine-one-one" on his hand-held cellular detonation keypad, the reaction sequence is initiated and within seconds, an explosion rips through an entire city block.

The bomb's rapid combustion sucks all of the air in and the lucky ones die instantly.

Less fortunate souls suffocate while melting flesh drips from their bones. When the smoke settles, a gruesome wrath of biblical proportions remains. Charred bodies take their places in smoldering graves as the cloistered ashes settle. There are no survivors.

The madman held the phone way above his head and with quivering hands and a trembling voice, he spoke to his chosen disciple. "Allah's blazing chariot will greet the retched non-believers who chastise the Merciful. As Jihad Time approaches our Prophet shall open his arms and welcome your inferno's ascension into Paradise."

Grateful tears rolled down the cheeks of the chosen one as he bowed his head, kneeled down, and kissed the feet of the Sheik.

Detective Francisco and Officer Landry kept scratching their heads and fishing for clues as they aimlessly combed the clinic for the third time. They went back to the station and looked at the drawing of satanic eyes and a crippled hand staring back down at them from the wall.

Francisco tore it off the wall, ran over to his desk, opened the bottom drawer, and grabbed a tattered black book containing hundreds of fax numbers. Police stations, fire stations, post offices, friends, informants, halfway houses, pool halls and strip joints. From his years on the force he was owed lots of favors. It was time to cash in. A glimmer of hope grinned through his languishing frown.

"Landry, start faxin' your ass off," said the detective, gesticulating wildly.

"Someone must have spotted the Sheik. He's a hard site to miss. Send this picture to everyone on this list." He scribbled a cover sheet that said: "I need your help. Find this man but do not approach him. Call me immediately. He is armed. He is dangerous. He has killed two innocent people. Don't be number three. Happy Thanksgiving. Detective Francisco."

When the faxes were sent, they drove to the clinic with a swat team, bomb squad, and explosive-sniffing dogs. The searched every square inch within two city blocks. They set up surveillance, snipers and roadblocks. They had to stop the Sheik. But stop him from what? They still did not know his plan. They drove across to the park with no choice but to sit and wait. It was eight a.m. It was silent. It was still, with a chill in the air.

Ha-med and Carole enjoyed room service on the terrace while cool ocean waves splashed the tranquil gray sky. All of a sudden, the scene came alive. A flock of seagulls began diving and soaring with pirouettes, flips, and a grand pas de deux. These skilled entertainers agreed to an encore with swoops, high dives and one last loop de loop. Then they curtsied and bowed and in choreographed motion and paused before fading off into the mist.

"What do birds believe in?" asked Carole.

With confidence, and without hesitation, Ha-med answered, "The Almighty."

Carole leaned against his warm naked chest, and as he kissed her neck, she said, "Mankind could learn much from those seagulls in the mist."

At ten o'clock an eerie silence hovered over the clinic. By ten-thirty, a dozen or so began assembling to partake in their best meal of the year. Photojournalists gathered to record clever politicians appearing to show how much they loved the poor. By eleven, Times Square on New Year's Eve would have seemed calm compared to the hordes converging upon the clinic's parking lot. A hot full course meal was worth standing in line for as the working-class poor, the unemployed, and the homeless gathered with huge appetites.

The ravenous commotion of raucous crowds drowned out the footsteps of Carole Meyer-Hassan as she stepped up to the platform and stood behind the podium. As she reached for the microphone, a high-pitched shrieking squeal of feedback quieted the noisy restless hungry crowds.

"Happy Thanksgiving, and welcome to the Cohen Clinic Annual Community Luncheon. Please be patient. We will be serving lunch in about an hour. There is plenty for everyone."

Volunteers negotiated their way up to join her. Aneesa rode on Ha-med's shoulders. Her head bobbed up and down like a toy puppy in a '55 Chevy's rear window. Her eyes were like vacuums as they sucked in the sights.

Construction equipment blocked off two main roads while detours and police whistles attempted to direct traffic's lethargic flow. David, Andrew, Sarah and the Ibrahims parked by the playground and the Imam and Afridi parked right behind them. The five caught up to Kahane and two other Chassidic Jews and they all strolled up together. Sheryl, Saul and the Rabbi trailed behind. Police escorts led them to the volunteers' platform. The roadblocks were ignored by the trusty old Ford whose clanking and clanging parted the crowds.

Francisco got out, paced up to the podium and gazed out at the swarms. He then looked back at Landry, frowned and shrugged his shoulders in a "still no sign of the Sheik" manner. Landry sat in the truck and peered out the windows with binoculars. As her eyes frisked the crowd, the outdated radio on the dashboard began squawking. She grabbed the mic and turned up the volume. Through the staticy speaker and noise of the crowd, she struggled to hear the police dispatch.

"Detective Francisco, this is base. Do you read me?"

"This is Officer Landry, we copy, go 'head."

"Some guy named Al says he got the fax, and needs to speak with Francisco. Says it's urgent. Do you copy? Urgent."

She slid out the driver's door, sprinted to the platform, told Francisco, and he flew back to the truck.

"This is Francisco. Go 'head."

"Al said you'd know who it is. He's on his cell. He said he'd wait for your call."

"Call him, and patch him through," said Francisco.

Alan Bambino, aka: "The Baby" was a stool pigeon Francisco had been using for years. He once was "connected" but when he decided to "come out of the closet," he was disowned. He was muscular, five foot ten with a roman profile, thick wavy hair, a black leather jacket and tight leather pants. His spoke New York Italian with a feminine flair.

"Detective, go ahead, he's on the line."

"Francisco? This is Bambino."

"So tell me you have some news for me," said the Detective.

"Those pic-chas ya faxed me that gave me the shivers? I'm gonna have nightmares for weeks."

"Al, tell me something I don't know."

"There's this fabulous building, used to be a fire station. We had a pole slidin' party there last Halloween."

"All right Al. Enough! I get the picture, I know the place, get on with it."

"That gothic lookin' guy wid the squished-up lookin' hand? Well, he checked in there a couple of days ago with two kids."

"Thanks Al, I owe you one."

"Promises, promises."

Francisco and Landry slingshotted out of the parking lot. While screeching their way westward, a law-abiding ambulance leisurely headed east. A traffic light caught the impatient detective; surrounded by cars, he was unable to run it.

Across the intersection, catty-cornered to his left and separated by pedestrians and automobiles was the ambulance bomb. When the light turned green, adrenalin fueled the good and the evil due east and due west.

Francisco parked a block away from the fire station. They ran over, and he snuck around back while Landry walked up to the front.

Guns drawn, they pounded on the doors. When nobody answered they shot out the locks and kicked their way in. The strong odor of gasoline filled a cold silent room and a big rental truck spewed the sick fumes of hate. Francisco went around to the back on the right; Landry on the left.

They hauled up the heavy door with a crash. Empty, except for a small heavy black iron case.

They pried open the case. Empty.

They searched the upstairs. Nothing.

From the vile stillness came a string of odd sounds. First a "ping" then and a "swoosh", then a repeating squeaky flapping sound, like an old rusty pendulum. It was coming from the restroom. While clutching their guns they surrounded the door, and kicked it open. A loud crash was followed by a cat's shrieking snarl as it knocked over the wastebasket and leaped out the window.

The mirror was fogged; the shower was wet; a bath towel was sloppily hung on a hook. Sitting by the sink was a washcloth, shaving cream, a razor, and a bottle of cologne. They inched their way down the row of five stalls. They stood off to the side, and with their guns drawn, one at a time, kicked open each door. Four in a row. Four empty stalls. Each one immaculate. Each looked unused.

They got to the last one on the left. It was larger than the rest, with a changing table, wheelchair-accessible. Francisco kicked the door, and grabbed his foot. The door was jammed; locked from the inside.

Landry crawled under.

"Hey Francisco, you gotta see this!"

She unlatched the door. The detective cringed and advanced. Hanging on a hook neatly arranged in an open garment bag staring straight at them was a Hollywood-quality disguise: a long flowing robe, a thick unkempt black beard, and a disheveled turban.

In synchronized motion Francisco and Landry looked at the get-up, looked at each other, flew out the door, jumped into his truck, and peeled away, oblivious to traffic. A few miles from the clinic they took a shortcut down a side street. They discovered too late it was closed for a street fair and they ignored anything that was blocking their way: furnishings, food vendors, florists and carts. They left a trail of rear end collisions as pedestrians, skateboarders and a mother with a stroller leaped onto the sidewalk and out of the way.

At ten minutes to Noon, Carole spoke again.

"Please form two lines and take your time," she paused for another short squeal of feedback, and continued, "There's plenty for all so please take your time. Be careful with small children. Assist the elderly and the infirmed. Have a happy and safe Thanksgiving lunch."

Professor Dahij strolled up and joined in the food-serving line with Arabs, Jews, an Imam, a Rabbi, Chassids, Hindus, blacks, whites,

Republicans, Democrats, rich and poor. Even Dr. Brennen waddled her way over to lend a hand.

Aneesa gave Dr. Dahij a loving smile.

"Hello Emit. Yep, I guess Allah willed it, 'cause here we are again."

He patted her on the head.

"Yes my little angel, happy Thanksgiving."

"Daddy, look at his Koran. It's just like yours, but yours is in better shape." Ha-med and Dahij smiled and winked at each other as Francisco and Landry bulldozed their way up to the front. Still nothing suspicious in site. They were concerned yet relieved.

"Keep your eyes on the crowd. I'm gonna stroll over to the park," said Francisco. He put a hand on Landry's shoulder.

"Landry, stay here. If you see anything suspicious, call me," The detective realized that everyone had a cell phone except him, so he snatched Carole's, and gave out the number as he headed towards the park.

"Everyone. Keep your eyes moving, ears tuned and minds focused," said Landry as she walked out amongst the masses.

With Aneesa on his shoulders, Ha-med joined the detective and strolled over to the park. Dr. Dahij and the Imam trailed right behind. Together they surveyed the park.

The crisp overcast autumn afternoon kept most people indoors. The deserted park hosted only the few who bundled up; braved the cold; and walked their dogs. A handful of birds and some squirrels kept them company.

Aneesa sat on the ground talking to the squirrels while the other four sat on the bench, eyes moving, hearts pounding, cell phones in hand. Every sound startled them. They decided to take shifts. Ha-med and the Imam took a walk while the detective and the professor remained on the bench. Aneesa sat next to the bench with her legs crossed, and admired the Koran in Dahij's hand. He clutched it tightly in one hand and his phone in the other.

The clinic was across the street to the left. The bench was at the park's entrance, with the playground to its right and picnic tables behind them.

Emit's head did not move. His sharp beady eyes beneath wire-framed glasses swept the entire scene like a metronome: clinic to park, clinic to park, clinic to park …

"May I now hold your Koran? I promise I'll be careful," said Aneesa.

His intense gaze toward the clinic rendered him temporarily oblivious to her existence. He noticed some action at the volunteer's station. The sudden commotion of converging crowds. The police were on it in no time at all and plain-clothed detectives shoved their way through. Carole was kneeling. Landry stood behind her. Her cell phone was beeping.

"Hey Landry, this is Francisco. What's happening over there? Is everything all right?"

"Yep. Everything is just fine. It's just Dr. Brennen. She's having a baby," said Landry.

"Oh great!" said Francisco. "She had to pick today?"

The emergency team managed to make their way through the crowds with a gurney, and carried her away. Carole stuck close by her side. Mr. Brennen was on his way, stuck in traffic.

"Breathe!" said Carole. "Sh-sh-sh. He-he-he. Remember what you tell your patients."

"C'mon Marjorie, you can do it. Hold on 'till we get inside!" said the E.R. doctor.

The sacrificial chariot began its approach. A clean-cut 20 year-old in a white lab coat and scrubs sat at the wheel. Proud, brave and anxious to accept his fate, he rolled down his window. As he approached the emergency entrance, impassible multitudes thwarted his path. A lane still remained from the emergency crew, but it was too narrow for the ambulance. His car slowed, his heart raced, his beads of sweat pooled. As he approached the crowd, the scene was reminiscent of Moses at the touch of his staff. The vast sea of feasters parted and the smiling swarms waved the ambulance on through.

Back at the park, still no sign of the Sheik. Dahij and Francisco sat on the bench while the Imam and Ha-med continued to pace. The Detective noticed the crowd motion and phoned Landry. "Hey Hon. Now what's happening?"

"Not much, lots of food, lots of people, Dr. Brennen's inside having her baby, some movement to let an ambulance through."

Aneesa realized that Dahij was intensely preoccupied, and did not hear her request to hold the Koran. She inched a little closer, uncrossed her legs, lifted herself up on her knees, and asked again.

"Hum … Hummm. I sure would like to hold your Koran."

Emit stared, mesmerized by his view of the clinic. The smoke from hot food in the crisp autumn sky was propelled like a cloud by the slow chilling breeze. He noticed the parting masses, and the ambulance. He squinted, and nodded his head to display his concern as he stared at the mobile phone in his left hand.

Aneesa misinterpreted his nod. She thought he was consenting to her request to see the Koran. Excited, she smiled, grabbed the sacred book with both hands and pulled it away.

With a high-voltage surge of fierce hostility, Emit Dahij whipped his head towards her with such speed that his glasses flew off the hook-nose of his beady-eyed face. As he leapt to his feet, his phone crashed on the ground.

With a horrified look and a shrill, piercing yelp, Aneesa put her hands on the ground behind her, dropped the Koran, and backed away on all fours.

She grabbed the Koran, clutched it to her chest, and froze in disbelief of what she saw next.

Lying between Dahij and Aneesa on a bed of fallen leaves was Dahij's left hand.

No blood. No cries of pain. Just a flawless left hand. Aneesa, trembling, backed up hard into a cold solid oak. She stared at the face of a shivering freak thinking his head was about to explode.

To Aneesa everything moved in slow motion, but the pause between heartbeats was all that had passed.

Detective Francisco witnessed the same scene, but from a different perspective. Hidden beneath the fine quality prosthetic hand was another, a real one, still attached at the wrist. This one had three fingers, scarred fingertips, and no fingernails.

Leaping to his feet, Francisco drew his weapon and fired twice at close range.

Emit Dahij came tumbling down. The bullet through his chest

may have missed Emit's heart, but the shot through his head sent the Sheik straight to hell.

As he hissed and he writhed like a tough wounded snake, he struggled to reach for his cellular phone. Sheik Khalil's last breath failed to press "nine-one-one," while Emit Dahij bid Aneesa farewell.

Epilogue

In a long-ago legend, a simple young woman, displeased with her appearance, was granted her wish. She then mothered a son whom she treated with kindness while many around him were heartless and cruel.

When his mother passed on he was left all alone.

The child was tugged in divergent directions: the love of his mother, barbaric regimes, virtuous thinkers, villainous schemes.

In his youth he survived an onslaught of misfortunes and his mind (like all minds) possessed evil and good.

He spent time with the righteous, as well as the sinful. Like a chameleon he learned to blend in with both sides.

His caravan rested one night in a village. He planted his seed and rode off before dawn. This man's bastard son was a prodigal-prodigy, who could never distinguish the just from the wicked.

As Jeckyl and Hyde hovered within his head, his nightmares were plagued by an internal struggle. His daytime delusions gnawed into his soul until both became one to his final demise.

The park grounds were cleared, the bomb was disarmed and The Cohen Clinic wound up with the finest ambulance money could buy. The deranged driver was handcuffed and hauled off to jail.

Dr. Brennen gave birth to a beautiful, eight-pound baby girl. She named her daughter Sabira.

Back at the station, Francisco and Landry tossed darts at the picture they'd returned to the wall. The detective walked into the locker room, emptied his pockets and washed his face.

On the edge of the sink sat his keys, some loose change, a cigarette lighter, a stick of chewing gum, and the crumpled paper he'd found on the desk at the warehouse. He unfolded the scribbled note, read it, scratched his head, and set it back down. Its mirrored reflection caught him off guard like the one-legged jump after stubbing one's toe. His reverberating yells echoed through the cold bathroom walls.

"Hey Landry, get your butt in here. Now!"

She couldn't imagine what could be so urgent. After making sure no one was watching, she shyly swung open the men's room door. "Hey Francisco. What's up?"

He looked spooked, shaken, and stunned. He spoke slowly, one word at a time like a first grade teacher to her reading class:

"**R e a d T h e S h e e t O f P a p e r**."

She looked at him strangely, thinking, no, knowing that he had been working to hard. She humored him. "Detective, the paper says Emit Dahij on top. Beneath it, it says, *when the upright and fallen come together, you will witness the guilty on that day linked together in chains. The names of the righteous are mirrored reflections whose evil sides hide in their minds eyes and words.*" She placed a hand on his back.

"Detective? Are you OK?"

He inhaled through his nose, held his breath for a moment and then exhaled slowly through his grinding teeth. He inhaled again.

"Mirrored reflections! Upright and fallen *together*? Mirrored reflections, eh?

R e a d T h e M i r r o r e d R e f l e c t i o n!"

She gazed at Francisco with a puzzled expression, shrugged her shoulders, and looked at the mirror. Officer Landry's perfectly sculpted nose and lips were surrounded by her fallen jaw and magnificent wide-opened eyes. She froze, suspended in time in a still-life's surreal eternity. On top of the paper, in neat large block letters, was the mirrored reflection of: "**E M I T D A H I J**." It said: "**J I H A D T I M E**."

She looked at Francisco. He closed his eyes, shook his head, and smirked. With a sarcastic smile, he said, "Officer Landry, how could *you* have possibly missed this?"He grabbed the paper, crumpled it into a wad, tossed it in the trash, and patted her on the back. With his arm on her shoulder, they walked out together to start their next case.

The weeks passed, and the celebrations of Christmas, Hanukkah, Dpavali and Ramadan were more appreciated than ever before. New Year's came and went, and the work at the Clinic continued as planned.

Stoltz had been gone and missed all the excitement but on his return they renamed the firm: "McDaniel, Stoltz and Hassan."

Detective Francisco got a computer, and in a chat room he introduced Rayne – the redhead with rings everywhere – to Richard, the techie. It was love at first pixel. Their wedding gift from Francisco was "Dawg."

David and Andrew spent the summer with Aneesa while Ha-med and Carole enjoyed their wedding gift from Kahane: A lavish vacation on his yacht with captain and crew. Shaina and Yoav met them in Athens, and together they cruised the Greek Islands.

The Hassan's returned from their trip. David and Andrew returned to their schools, and Aneesa started the first grade.

Late one night Aneesa had a nightmare, so she snuck in and snuggled between Ha-med and Carole. In the morning, the three awoke to soothing Neil Diamond songs on the radio. Another glorious day. Time for school, time for work.

They stretched, yawned, hugged, and gazed out the window. It was without a doubt, the most magnificent morning in years. A brilliant blue sky, no chance of showers and the temperature was perfect. As the song faded, the DJ cut in.

"I hope you guys enjoyed Neil Diamond's *September Morn'* here on KGSB in New York City.

As we continue our oldies but goodies countdown, the next one up is The Rascal's: *Beautiful Mornin'.*

"And a beautiful morning it is here in New York City at 7:35 a.m. The sun's shinning bright, and the weather's near perfect.

"So go play hooky or call in sick. Take a family day for a stroll through the park or go toss a Frisbee and have a picnic. Whatever you do, have a fabulous day this Tuesday, September 11, 2001."

Printed in the United States
20774LVS00002B/1-24